the deliberate
SINNER

the deliberate SINNER

bhaavna arora

Srishti
PUBLISHERS & DISTRIBUTORS

SRISHTI PUBLISHERS & DISTRIBUTORS
N-16, C. R. Park
New Delhi 110 019
editorial@srishtipublishers.com

First published by
Srishti Publishers & Distributors in 2014
Fifth impression 2014

Printed and bound in India

Dedicated to
my readers

Acknowledgements

Yes, I'm a dreamer like most of us. But the dream of a book taking the present form of *The Deliberate Sinner* would never have been possible if I didn't have the motivation and encouragement from a few to be mentioned.

I would like to thank Prof Surindra Lal for the pain he took with my first edits.

The entire team at Srishti deserves a special mention for they worked very hard to give the book its final shape.

I would like to thank my friends Talvinder, Priyanka, Itee, Thakur, Sriram and Raadha for believing in my dreams and being honest critics.

I would like to mention Deepti auntie and Divya Prakash Mallya auntie for their spiritual support. Dr Parmar uncle's suggestion of not giving up did much good to my spirits.

Last but not the least, my family, for always letting me be…at my will. Especially my mother who made sumptuous sandwiches for me, even at 4 in the morning, while I wrote.

And most importantly, to all the readers for picking up the book and encouraging me with their honest feedback and suggestions.

Prologue

'**I**'ve been a soldier all my life, and I have defended my nation with the same devotion with which I have tended to my family,' the grand old man was enfeebled by pneumonia, but his spirits were high. Rihana's grandfather had been a fighter, but he now seemed to be losing the battle to his stressful breaths and the tears sparkling in his dainty granddaughter's eyes.

Rihana sensed that these could be her last moments with the 'best man' of her life. In such a situation, where pain is excruciating and unbearable, death becomes a welcome panacea.

Her grandfather, who she lovingly called Dadu, had been a very positive person. For him, no problem was bigger than its solution, and that's how Rihana had picked up that trait. How could she not; she had grown up watching him move mountains with his nonchalant attitude. She could hear him sharing his mantra with her when she was still little: *You have to take the problem head on. Either you die, or you kill your enemy; there is no other way.*

Rihana was adored by her grandfather because the lessons given to her were not merely heard; they lay enshrined in the deepest recesses of her heart. He witnessed her practicing his ideas in her daily routine, and that made his chest swell in pride. Whether it was an academic failure or an adolescent love failure, it was like falling off a horse's back and she had to get right back on because if she fell on her back, she would only see upside. That position is best in one's grave but not when one has to get on with life.

Her reverie was broken with the sudden movement of his fingers. When he rolled his eyes towards his hand, Rihana saw the multiple tubes connected to monitors through his hand and fingers. He must be feeling pain, she thought. She slid her hand under his to divert his attention from the pain.

He mustered strength from it and continued, 'You know, when you were a little girl, I would ferry you around the city on my scooter. But you would first stand in front of the scooter's side mirror to check yourself out.' She could see a faint smile spreading across his eyes, 'Decked up in a *salwar-kameez* with a small *bindi* sparkling on your broad forehead…the same bindi that you kept taking from your dadi's cupboard, with the poor woman wondering where all her bindis went. If ever I drove the scooter a bit faster than usual, you would create a fuss and ask me to slow down lest your bindi flew off.'

She had a hazy memory of this, but her dadi had narrated this incident enough times for her to know it by heart now. Her tinkling laughter and his smile made the ambience a little less tense.

It was then that the brave old man began talking incoherently about something. Rihana could only catch bits of his words; his speech was slurred. She gathered after great effort that he wanted his decorations from the Army, an array of his meticulously organized medals in a wooden frame hung on the wall of his living room, to be handed over to her father.

She did not understand the purport and was perplexed by her grandfather's wish. But she did not question, and instead, listened to him patiently.

This time when he spoke, his penetrating glance held her. He had looked into her soul through his round glasses for years now, especially every time he thought she was hiding pain within her. 'I understand you've gone through hell, my child. But then, this is what life is. The day you stop experiencing pain or pleasure, that very day you would cease to exist. Pain and pleasure are inseparable.' He paused to catch his failing breath, and Rihana got a chance to swallow the lump forming in her throat. 'And in the interlude between birth and death, it's your deeds alone that make the story of your life – either remarkably big or abysmally insignificant.'

Though Rihana was at a loss to decipher the context of her grandfather's enigmatic remarks, he continued, 'I had always wished this for you, Rihana. A plan, which was overruled by your destiny. Even birds fly in pairs. They gather strength from each other….'

Rihana understood. She wanted to look away, but his gaze held hers hypnotically. His eyes had brimmed with tears, 'I would love to see you paired, but only with someone you can love. If you're not happy, don't waste time in confusion, for confusion is not a good place to dwell in.'

Barely had he finished that he lost his breath and the monitors beeped. He was struggling to breathe. The nurses rushed in and asked Rihana to step out. She pulled back her hand reluctantly and stood at a distance, seeing the two nurses in action. He had calmed down after a few seconds.

She pulled herself out of the room and crashed on the chair. The empty corridor seemed painfully quiet, with just the unsettling beep emanating from the room where her 'best man' lay, probably breathing his last. She knew too well that nothing but her pain could have beaten his positivity. She felt troubled with her grandfather's last wish.

Soaring High

*R*ihana had carefully chosen a baggy overall a couple of sizes too large for herself. She had been planning and looking forward to this day for some time now. As she stepped up on a portable ladder and picked up the brush dripping a vibrant pink into the bucket hanging on the side of the ladder, she flashed a broad smile. She had heard many men, and even women, compliment her on her enigmatic, colourful smile. She was going to use the same colour of happiness for redecorating the walls of her house today. With time, life had sapped all colour out of her life, and she was set to re-do it, in her way now.

She squeezed the extra paint off the brush on the sides of the bucket and looked up to see where to begin. She had to start from higher up to avoid any paint from trickling down unnecessarily. She was still formulating her thoughts, oblivious to the tall, broad, well-built man who had sneaked up behind her. Only when she started to paint, he lifted her off the ladder with ease, and she shrieked as the brush kissed the floor instead of the walls. She was first in a state of shock, followed with surprise by the gesture of the man who had his arms tight around her waist, and her feet dangling mid-air…that's how he carried her to the bedroom. The urgency with which he put her down and turned her to face him pushing her to the wall of the bedroom, she knew he wanted her. He held her close, in a grip that almost crushed her into him. It was in a split second that his mouth sought hers. Though flummoxed by the suddenness, Rihana welcomed him.

Veer had locked his fingers in Rihana's as his tongue locked into hers too, each exploring the confines of the other's mouth eagerly. When he forced her arms behind her fiercely, she was in pain. But the pain only accentuated her craving. Veer pulled her to him again, his hands locked into hers behind her back, aiding his movement. The incessant kissing, and their worked-up tongues flirting with each other was all it took for Rihana to be flooded with passion. She was moving to Veer's rhythm, as if performing a tango with the music of their hearts beating loud. She could feel him against her belly now, hard in his trousers. He let go of her hands and lifted her up to spread her on the bed. In his eagerness, he tore off a few buttons and hurriedly stripped the overall off to feast his eyes on her. This wasn't the Veer Rihana knew. It was also the first time ever that she saw him look at her with admiration.

Veer was mesmerized by her. He shifted his gaze from the delicious curves of her waist to the beautifully scooped navel from where a thin stream of brown hair emerged to spread into a velvety carpet between her ivory white thighs. A charm pendant in her waistband played mischievously on the brown carpet, occasionally kissing her valley seductively. Her shapely calves were provocatively alluring; her angelic feet just divine.

Veer had taken in each bit of her hungrily. And now, as adrenaline pumped faster in his blood, he nose-dived into her valley and started caressing her nub with his tongue. Rihana was now moaning in sheer ecstasy, and on cue dug her fingers into his hair, gently prodding him deeper. It was a little difficult for Rihana to accept such a drastic change. But her eyes reflected a craving; a desire of the mind that had gradually changed into the desire of the body. Her body was starved, and so was her soul. She knew too well that beggars could not be choosers, so she exulted in whatever came her way.

Veer looked up at her; her hunger was reflected in his eyes as well. Rihana unbuttoned his trousers and Veer quickly undressed himself and lay on top of her. He made her lie on her stomach and slithered upward from her back. He knew too well how sensitive her nape was and how it could take her to the edge in no time. He soon heard the moans go wild and felt her want reaching a crescendo. He rolled her to face him and ate at her ample breasts, the most bewitching part of her body. Despite being buxom, they were firm and seductive. Her nipples were blooming and supple and when he fervently kissed and savoured their nectar, she was aroused to further heights of ecstasy. She was now dripping and Veer could feel her juices and the thirst for a gala celebration. He reached down to her warmth and rubbed her sensitive spot, making her moan louder. To keep the loud moans in check, he sealed her mouth with his. He continued to play his magical fingers on her nipples and she herself took charge of her reservoir of happiness, her clit. She stroked it as Veer took care of her mouth and ample breasts till she shuddered into an orgasm. That was the third time in three months that Veer had been generous enough to give her one.

She was still panting in the afterglow when Veer moved. She knew well what was to follow and did not object. In fact, she wanted to please him with even more intensity and slid downward to take his hardness in her mouth. She knew how men enjoyed this part of the eleven minute process; thanks to all the porn she had watched. Just after the very first stroke, Veer seemed hesitant. He rolled her on the bed and came on top of her. Probably he didn't want another fiasco. He slowly spread her legs, and glided into her depth with ease for she was overflowing with her own juices. In a few passionate strokes, she was moving to Veer's rhythm and was transported into bliss with her man inside her. He came out as quickly as he had gone in. But this time Rihana didn't curse him, as he had been generous enough to grant her wish first. She wasn't left hanging in between.

Rihana was among those few women who knew what an orgasm was and how to explode into it. It was a blessing, as a transcendental experience of cosmic order. She had come to understand it as a way to spirituality, unison with oneself, and most importantly, a feeling of being human. Men, by default, are more prone to experiencing an orgasm, but surely it can't be restricted to only men. If a woman who is aware of an orgasm doesn't reach it, it turns out to be a curse for her.

In his utter ingrained chauvinism, coupled with callousness, Veer like most men was impervious to a woman's needs.

Rihana was a puppet and Veer played with her body and made it dance to his tune... only when he wanted. But Rihana had needs that were never satisfied. As he lay next to her, peacefully dosing into a siesta, she lay wide awake, thinking.

♀

Rihana had planned a trip to Thailand with her friends, but when eventually she had hopped on to the flight, she was all alone. The destination was chosen on a special criterion too: Thailand was the only country that she was not allowed to visit by her parents. 'The country whose economy is based on and debased by prostitution... a woman has no business there. What would you do in a country like that?' She assumed her friends had met the same reaction and had, thus, backed out. But this did not keep her from what she had decided to do. She planned to go alone.

Rihana's father, Rajendra Bajwa, was a well-known Punjabi businessman who owned three marble mines in Jaipur. Her mother, on the other hand, was a local politician exercising considerable say and control over local matters. As one would gather, they had money coming out of their ears, and time slipping out of their hands. Being their only child, Rihana enjoyed their undivided attention, till the attention became an obsession. Her father was neck deep in managing his business and detached in certain ways, but a responsible man nonetheless. He took care of the family in monetary terms and all else it could buy. Rihana's mother didn't have any problems with Mr Bajwa's non-availability for two reasons: she had learnt to compromise, and she treated money as her second husband. Time was a luxury Mr Bajwa could not afford in parenthood. Rihana's mother, on the other hand, had all the time in the world. She used most of it to cultivate changes in Rihana which would make her socially more acceptable and wanted. She was a public figure, and had mastered the art of going from being the most wonderful person to the most embarrassing one in a blink. What else would someone think when she called Rihana by her nick name, *Totta* in front of others. It is a north-Indian slang word for a sexy woman, and she hated being called that by everyone, especially by her mother. That word could encourage others to misuse it. No one knew why and how she got that name, but the only person from whom others got to know about it was her mother who invariably called her by that name, in public too.

Rihana often wondered if her mother realised that the word had derogatory connotations, that of a woman being an object that could be owned rather than someone to be cherished. Maybe that's why Rihana detested that name and considered it demeaning.

So her mother, totally oblivious of the name she called her daughter by and very conscious of the effect of Rihana's trip to Thailand on their family status had confronted her, 'What sort of a girl goes to Thailand alone, Totta? It's so unsafe for you to travel unaccompanied.'

'Mom, stop calling me that if you want me to listen to you. And tell me if I should take Roop Chand along?' Rihana said in a polite, yet sarcastic tone.

Roop Chand had been Rihana's driver-cum-bodyguard ever since she could remember. Although Rihana drove pretty well herself, Roop Chand ferried her in a Mercedes E-550 coupe gifted to her by her mother on her twenty-first birthday. Roop Chand was more of an ally for her, who played hand in glove in all her pranks. When Rihana was in school, Roop Chand would go to drop her and pick her up. On her way to school, she would try her hands on her father's car, under Roop Chand's eagle eye. She had seen a lot of women depending on the men in their family for being driven around, and had also come to see this as a standard way in the male-dominated society to throw their weight around. Some women wanted it that way, so that they could treat their husbands as couth chauffeurs, but most of them were denied the privilege of being independent. A man owning a car, a woman and a gun was considered truly masculine. And women were only supposed to get married to such men and become their possessions.

For Rihana, the ideals of manhood were manifested when men let their women drive them around. It wasn't about gender equality, but of a man's confidence to wear his caring and emotional side on his sleeves, proudly baring it for all to see. There wasn't anything sexier than a man who was confident enough to let his woman take over. Roop Chand had helped her in that first lesson which had enabled her to stand strong for her ideas.

She was beyond doubt born with a silver spoon and the money definitely made living life on her own terms a cinch. She had graduated in International Management from the Franklin College in Switzerland, one of the most beautiful countries she had ever seen. But her mother had forced her to come back after graduation, to be with her so that she could have more of her daughter. She had returned reluctantly and enrolled for her Master's in Jaipur.

'You know, Mom, all my friends have backed out. I am sure their parents must have overreacted.' And then she started counting each point on her fingertips dramatically, in a sing song voice at that, more for a cumulative effect than to keep count of the reasons. You and Dad never have enough time to finish off your professional jobs, leave aside holidaying with your daughter. I don't have a boyfriend. I don't have any siblings.' Then she looked up and hit the nail on the head, 'It would've been nice if you and Dad had thought of giving me a younger brother or sister. It's completely your fault that you did not prevent Dad from using protection back then, or I would have had company to go to Thailand today.'

She had said all of it in such mock innocence that it took her mother some time to take note of what had just passed. Rihana, meanwhile, was reminded of her teenage memory of finding a packet of condoms in her father's shaving kit while searching for a nail clipper. They didn't even burst with a full bucket of water. Must be quality ones, she presumed when she had taken a few to her school and used them as water balloons. She snapped back to reality with her mother's raised voice.

'What nonsense is this, Rihana? Behave yourself!' rebuked Rihana's mother, who somehow had always felt guilty for not having a second child, someone to give Rihana a sense of sharing. Dogs and children at home are always preferred in pairs, someone had told her back then, though she didn't remember who. In pairs, they are generally a lesser nuisance, for they stay busy fighting, playing and entertaining each other.

Her mother gathered herself and knew that she had hit the dead end of the argument with her daughter. There was no option but to relent. 'I won't allow you more than a week and make sure that I have all the details of your bookings in Thailand,' commanded Rihana's mother.

Rihana knew she would be able to pull it off; her mother had given in quite easily. She squealed in excitement and gave her a peck on the cheek before running out of the house to call out to Roop Chand for getting her tickets done.

Roop Chand was equally excited; with Rihana away, he would have ten days to himself. He had known it ever since Rihana came up with this travel idea that she will pull it off. Rihana worked against the current almost always, and he had never seen her give up till date. Moreover, he had been Rihana's ally ever since she was three years old. One could say he had literally brought her up. Her parents were required to attend formal events very often, and he was the most sincere and trusted worker of the family. Who else could they leave Rihana to; the man who knew what would make their daughter tinkle in happiness at any time was their obvious preference. He was at Rihana's service for any task, ever since.

Roop Chand started with making arrangements for her travel – from tickets to accommodation to an entire itinerary that Rihana had drafted for him, and all was very well taken care of. It was promptly approved by her parents who knew Roop Chand would never let a loophole linger into any plans for Rihana. On the day of the travel as well, he dropped Rihana at the airport and shot a thumbs up as she entered the airport to stand at the end of the long queue.

She wondered where all these people were off to in the middle of the night. While in the queue, she was doing a last minute check of her travel gear and suddenly realized that she had left her headphones in the car. She took out her mobile phone from the pocket of her jacket, and speed dialled her man Friday.

She literally screamed,'Roop Chand, come back! I forgot the headphones.' She disconnected the call but till then, half the people ahead of her and many around her were staring at her, wide-sleepy-eyed. She ignored them all and walked towards the exit, telling the middle-aged man behind her that she will be back to take her place in a jiffy.

Roop Chand, on the other hand, was quite used to this drill. And his surety of this happening every single time was so much that when she walked towards the exit, she saw Roop Chand standing there already, with her headphones and her travel pillow in his hands. She collected her things, flashed the usual 'you-know-me' smile, and got back in the queue.

When the crawling queue *finally* took her to the check-in counter, she had all documents in place, and a special request for a window seat.

'Miss, anything else that I can help you with?' the ground staff member asked courteously.

'Just make sure a good looking guy sits next to me,' she smiled. Her grandfather had once told her that a smile with thank yous and sorrys had the potential to change the world around, slowly, but steadily. Little did she know that this smile to the staff at the airport would really change her life.

Rihana boarded the plane and looked for her seat, only to find a tall, handsome man sitting next to her. Grandpa's idea worked! She settled down in her seat and put her bag below the seat in front of her.

It would be wrong to say that the man travelling to Thailand, sitting next to this gorgeous girl was not interested in striking a conversation with her. But Rihana was clearly more interested in her book. She presumed the ground staff had taken her joke about the good looking co-passenger rather seriously.

'Hi! Are you travelling alone?' was how he broke the ice.

She looked at him in utter annoyance and said, 'So are you!'

'No, I'm not. I'm travelling with a group of friends. They are sitting at the back.' His smile was his first victory over Rihana, subtle and warmly slicing through the ice.

He then introduced himself as Veer Singh Rathore. She had definitely heard the surname somewhere, she thought. He went on to elaborate about his father's real estate business in Jaipur, Delhi and Mumbai, fairly certain that it would establish him as a 'good guy'. Rihana kept her conversations with Veer restricted till the plane landed. Once she put her feet on the ground, Veer introduced Rihana to his friends – Raj More and Ravi Poonia.

Rihana looked at Raj for a few seconds too long before screaming in sheer disbelief, 'Why didn't you tell me that you were planning a trip to Thailand? We could have planned it together.'

Raj didn't know what to say, so he just smiled sheepishly. Veer, on the other hand, hit Raj with an extremely questioning glance and quickly shifted his now softened gaze to Rihana, 'Oh! So both of you know each other?'

'Yes! We're best buddies and swimming partners,' replied Rihana.

Veer was drawn to Rihana instantly and was thinking of ways to be with Rihana in Thailand. But his friends were not overly thrilled with that idea, and Rihana had no such plans.

In a place like Bangkok and Pattaya, nobody wanted to hang out with one girl. There was a variety of women all around and the boys were going to pick the best ones. Rihana had her itinerary of adventure sports and shopping in place and didn't want her plans to be disrupted. Rihana was not oblivious to Veer's wishes, thanks to his overflowing facial expressions, but chose to stick to her plans.

Rihana had a good time in Bangkok, because she shopped herself almost bankrupt, and got body massages in Pattaya – the city that offered one of the best massages in the world. The massage parlours at Walking Street were a hub for prostitution, and Rihana was awe-struck at witnessing the booming 'industry' from so close. She did not have any such inclinations but the men coming to Pattaya definitely did not mind. She learnt from her friendly masseuse that for a mere three hundred Indian rupees, men could get a stimulating 'massage', on the right places of their anatomy. Rihana was first exposed to this when she heard a man in a massage room next to hers moan in ecstasy. She exchanged looks with her masseuse who was rolling her eyes; both of them had broken into giggles together.

'A man is the weakest after his erection and before his spurt. That's when we raise our prices,' said the masseuse winking at Rihana, who was rather amused at the unabashed exclamation.

'And I'm so sure that as you negotiate higher prices, their Eiffel towers must be changing to dried mushrooms!' Rihana's comment unleashed a burst of loud laughter. This also eased the scope of a conversation between them. After her interaction with the masseuse, Rihana realized how unhappy that young girl was with her job, and probably wanted someone to rescue her forever. Though there were definitely some women like her who did get lucky, but most of them hung on to their jobs for survival. It was quick money, no doubt, but definitely not easy. These women had learnt to exploit one of the three Ls – Land, Loot and Lady – that has been most desired by men all along. When they could fight wars over these, spending money was fairly easy. The government had done its share by regulating such services in order to give their economy the much-required boost. She thought, Hadn't Switzerland done a similar thing by allowing people to keep their loot safe in their country! No wonder Indians top the list of visitors to both these countries.

She wondered what prostitution had done to these women, except having reduced the most cherished intimacy between two people to a mere commodity that could be traded. These questions haunted Rihana and she wondered at the fate of such women in her own country. More than that, she was perplexed at how women had commodified themselves for survival, pushed to such means for the lack of any other option.

But she was in Thailand to enjoy, and enjoy she did! Rihana tried her hands at everything from para-sailing to banana boat rides, from all-terrain-vehicles to sky diving and deep sea diving... She enjoyed every bit of the adventure, and felt the few minutes that she spoke to her mother over phone every day had weighed longer than her week-long holiday.

When she returned to Jaipur a week later, Rihana recited the stories of her adventures in Thailand to her mother. Her mother kept telling her that the last time Rihana was this excited narrating something was perhaps when she had recited the story of *Alice in Wonderland*. She had been seven years old then, and now old enough to know what to censor out of the Thailand story.

Prince Charming??

Rihana was rejuvenated after the holiday and valued her independence slightly more than earlier. She returned to the grind of helping her father in his business in the mornings and continued her swimming sessions every evening – one of the many activities she would passionately involve herself in. She was a district level swimmer with gold and silver medals telling tales of her accomplishments. She had also been fascinated with colours and fabrics all along. Although she was not really interested in the family business, she helped her father for the sheer need of the hour. She had learnt some skills with her formal education that she thought would benefit her father's business. But deep deep down, she was obsessed with fabrics, colours, textures and designs. She had been coaxing her father to branch out into non-marble ventures, but he was reluctant and too busy to experiment. She wanted to learn how her father managed a huge business to be able to start one up on her own when she was ready.

She was treated as a trainee in office by her father who wanted her to be a humble learner. Since everyone else in the office saw her as the heir, all the expectations made it a strenuous combination for her. Nonetheless, her evenings were joyful, thanks to the swimming schedule. She preferred walking from her house to the club nearby, and crossed the tennis court to reach the pool. This was a major event in the lives of the guys playing tennis. It was a morale booster of sorts for them, as each player would serve and hit better, with louder sporty grunts. A beautiful and fashionable girl with a short-skirt hugging her shapely thighs worked like a catalyst for an instant adrenaline rush. She, out of habit, never turned to look at the players; even if she happened to and caught someone's eyes on her, she would exchange a cursory smile and walk past. The object of her smile would indulge in some histrionic or the other to catch her attention. And she briskly walked past, rolling her eyes, at a loss to handle all this attention.

Summer evenings saw most members throb around the pool for relief, making it difficult to find adequate space. Rihana took a corner and glided from one end towards the other. While she was moving her arms and legs rhythmically to complete the twenty-lap target she had set for herself, floating on the cool blue waters, she realized someone's intense gaze on her. She stopped at the nineteenth lap, because the man's look was pretty gripping and unsettling.

'Rihana, how can you swim so well?' It was Veer! She later came to know that he had enquired about her from Raj and had ended up in the same club, at the same time, doing the same thing as her.

She wondered what he was up to, but the jovial bounce in her persona made her quip with a cheeky smile and laden innuendo, 'Swimming is for youth that are overflowing with raging hormones. It helps to burn excess energy in the pool, or the population of our country will multiply manifold over this summer.'

She dived back to complete her twentieth lap, and got out from the other end of the pool from where Veer was. After nodding and saying hello to a few acquaintances she met at the pool almost every day, she walked away to take a shower. She was forced to think back on Raj, the only close friend Rihana could completely trust, and what Veer could have said to extract all this information about her out of him. Though she was well aware that he had a soft corner for her in his heart, but she felt safe in his company and his intelligent conversations and wit gave her a high.

Rihana and Raj were buddies. He was a Maharashtrian staying in Jaipur. He was as brawny as a bull and dark complexioned enough to give anyone's confidence a sound blow. But he laughed it all off. In fact, he often joked how he could have served as a great contender for the lead role in the chewing gum advertisement in which they used a buffalo and sparkling white teeth to great effect.

Rihana remembered the day she had accompanied Raj for he had to buy a new suit for an official party. Since he was more confident of Rihana's styling than his own, he asked her to come along and she happily obliged. They ended up zeroing down on a black suit, after which Raj's insistence on buying a white shirt irked Rihana. Sensing the fast approaching breakdown point in his partner, Raj blurted, 'If I wore this suit at night, it would be hard to spot me in the dark.'

Listening to his self-depreciating remark, she had burst into a joyful laughter.

Raj had the skill to make her laugh; even at his own cost. She was surprised how he had a satirical joke for every occasion. Rihana loved his company and since Raj never took advantage, she was very comfortable with him. Since they were seen together most times, they had come to be called 'Ebony & Ivory' in Jaipur.

Pretty girls confided in men like Raj for four reasons: first, they are harmless; second, they cannot be mistaken as some pretty girls' boyfriend; third, girls are saved to a certain extent from frivolous gossip as no one would ever think they were a couple; and finally, girls enjoyed undivided attention from such men.

The men's dressing room was right next to the women's and voice permeated through the thin walls with ease. While women were usually too loud themselves to pay heed to what men were saying, Rihana knew that the men gossiped as much as the ladies. And she knew well, men who gossiped were probably nastier than the women. The dominant topic of discussion in the men's room was the girls' physique, and Rihana's long, shapely legs. There were times Rihana wondered why these men were obsessed with legs. That part of her anatomy was discussed the most, as if that was all there was to her. And since that was the only bit their eyes could see, the rest was left to their wild conjecturing till they ran amok.

Rihana moved out of the dressing room after a shower, and found Veer waiting to speak to her. Seeing her walk towards her house, he offered to drop her home. Chivalry was, after all, not dead; it just worked to cover ulterior motives now.

The only purpose that Rihana could see was promotion – from discussing about her legs to actually spreading them. She had seen men behave like vulnerable puppies for that, and this seemed like just another addition. Rihana carried a devil-may-care attitude, and when combined with an overt sexuality, it attracted her ardent lovers. She had been used to such proposals and declined it with even more chivalry, 'Thank you, Veer! I trust my legs to carry me home safely.'

Aware of the talk in the men's dressing room – thanks to Raj – she whispered in an evil tone, 'These legs haven't spread for anyone, and I don't intend for them to betray me.'

It didn't take any time for Veer to decipher what she had just let slip; he was a sharp young man. He thought himself to be the virtual owner of Rihana's legs, and also understood that Rihana meant what she had just said. She was not going to be easy.

Veer belonged to a Rajput family of Jaipur, and as they say, had the blood of warriors run in him. His father owned a real estate business and most of the marble used on their construction sites was procured from Rihana's father's mines. Both the families knew each other, but Rihana wasn't aware of that. She had just entered the business and was mainly handling the accounts. She had probably never met Veer till now because he had just returned from New York after completing architectural engineering. He had now joined his father's booming business and was working hard to spread it further beyond its current expanse in Jaipur, Delhi and Mumbai.

Veer met Rihana again the next day, at the same place, and asked her out for a cup of coffee. 'Veer, I respectfully decline the invitation to join your hallucination,' she said politely, quoting Scott Adams.

The look on Veer's face was that of a little boy whose ice-cream had just been snatched. And it was for the same reason that he was drawn towards Rihana; hard-to-get girls are more desirable to men.

Veer had been pushed away by Rihana way too many times, but his instinct told him she was marriage material: good looking, educated, smart, and yet unrelenting to just about any Tom, Dick or Harry. What he needed to do was...be special.

It is astonishing how men can differentiate between marriage material and *fille de joie* material. Women for them are multiple choice questions, and they pick the choice that suits the situation.

Veer's situation pushed him into pursuing this girl, who he thought would fit his and his family's needs perfectly. So the next day was even more interesting for the impatient Rajput who refused to give up. Rajputs had been a fighter clan in the past, and he would hold up to that fame till he won this battle.

Next evening, just as Rihana was about to start her twenty lap marathon in the swimming pool, Veer gathered his plan and asked her, 'How many laps do you do in a day?'

Raj was settled within earshot and turned towards Rihana in anticipation of a crisp reply for his dear friend.

'Twenty,' said Rihana with a sense of pride, without looking at Veer.

'That is quite a lot...,' Raj said impressed, but was soon cut short by Veer.

'If one really wants it, even a hundred is nothing,' Veer exhorted boastfully.

Rihana and Raj shared a he-is-bluffing look and Rihana got back to her laps.

'Can you do it?' Raj came straight to the point with Veer.

'Even if I can, why should I?' He smiled mischievously at Raj and continued, 'If I am promised a reward for it, then maybe I can think about it. Rihana stopped in between and looked at Veer with challenge writ large on her face.

Veer looked straight into her eyes and said softly, 'If Rihana agrees to go out for a cup of coffee with me, I will.'

Rihana looked at Raj who smiled and nodded in affirmation. Raj was pretty confident Rihana would not have to go with Veer.

'And what if you lose Veer?' Raj prodded.

'Whatever you say, dude,' retorted Veer.

'Well, then you can take *me* out for a cup of coffee, or dinner or whatever else you had in mind. Let's work on a "retain the plan, replace the partner" strategy,' responded Raj with a straight face.

That tête-à-tête between Veer and Raj drove Rihana into peals of laughter. She had somehow started imagining Raj and Veer on a date and couldn't hold on to her horses after that. Her laughter was always loud and contagious, and her grandma had always taunted her, 'Nobody will marry you if you laugh like this. Laugh like a girl!'

She had often wondered at her grandma's admonition how even laughter could victimize girls. But for this moment, she laughed with abandon and completed her twenty laps before perching on the poolside to count Veer's.

Veer started from zero mark at 4 p.m. and reached the eighty-second lap at 8 p.m. Rihana was now worried, not from the fear of losing the bet, but from the fear that Veer might collapse in the pool. She asked him to stop at the eighty-second lap and agreed to go out with him. But he looked at it as a challenge to his ego more than his physical capacity and completed the hundred laps. That proved, more than his stamina, his strong will to get Rihana. Raj's presence was acting as a constant stimulus and making Veer's will stronger. He would prove to Raj what he could do for some time with Rihana.

Raj hugged him when Veer finally came out of the pool. Rihana smiled softly and held out her hand to congratulate him. Veer was quick to hold her hand and bend down on one knee to proclaim, 'All this wasn't for a cup of coffee with you, Rihana. Will you marry me?' asked Veer exhibiting his Rajput impatience.

Raj's smile vanished for a moment as Rihana looked at him in surprise; both hadn't seen this coming. But as Raj broke into a smile and moved away from the pool to give them some space,

Rihana smiled mildly. 'What a romantic proposal over hundred laps of a fifty-metre pool,' marvelled Rihana. She held his hand and pulled him up on his feet. With a soft smile playing on her lips, she picked up her things and went back home.

She had just completed her studies, was barely twenty-one and tender, innocent and inexperienced in the matters of the heart. She was not a good judge of people, but luckily, was also aware of this.

Rihana was not sure what to make of the proposal. Veer could have been bluffing, he could have been serious; she knew she was too young to be married, but Veer didn't seem too bad a guy. She also thought her parents would want a good match for her soon, then what was the harm in picking up a guy she already knew!

She came home and sat in the living room caressing her black Labrador retriever named Caesar. He was her companion for a few years now and both adored each other equally. She streamlined her thoughts and acquainted her parents with Veer's proposal on the dinner table. Her otherwise sophisticated mother would have been excited enough to squeal with a full mouth, 'Oh! That real estate company owner's son!' Her mother was excited without even seeing or knowing the boy.

Most Indian families are predictable in their ways of finding a well-settled groom for their daughters. 'Well settled' in Indian context would mean the boy being financially independent and sound, offering stability and a decent living. Good looks, qualities, capabilities, et al., were the icing on the cake. Certain other fundamentals like physical, mental and emotional compatibility are ignored in lieu of financial standing, making it a tricky affair.

Rihana's understanding of a marriage came from her witnessing the mechanical bond between her parents, which scared her. Inevitably, she dreamed of a perfect marriage, where her companion would complete her. Little did she know then that marriage, albeit expected to be a perfect bond, is the most perfect only in its imperfections.

Her parents took it upon themselves to take it from there and Rihana was promptly given a backseat after asking if she liked Veer. She did not dislike him, and that had been enough for her family, because they felt, 'Love could be arranged'.

So, the next day, Rihana's mother spoke to Veer and arranged for the families to meet. The families met within the next couple of days, first at Rihana's house, then at Veer's. There were no hiccups in the families fixing them up together, but it did leave Rihana perplexed because everything happened in a frenzy and sick hurry. It seemed as if overnight, her independent, carefree and self-contained life was going to change. She had butterflies in her stomach for marriage was a big thing, but also conflict, confusion and some amount of rage in her mind.

Rihana held herself back from discussing things with the heartbroken Raj, her only true friend, whose liking for Rihana had met a dead end with the news of her marriage. The thought of marriage of one's beloved has spawned many a Devdas. The remedy giver was more in pain than the remedy seeker.

Rihana and Raj gradually came to terms with the fact that the former was losing more than her independence to the man she didn't know and the latter was losing the former.

The engagement ceremony was announced to confirm the alliance between the girl and the boy, more so between two affluent families. The two girls to save Rihana the woes of a quick alliance turned up for the ceremony from Delhi. Tamanna and Richa had done their graduation with Rihana in Switzerland

and had contributed in Rihana's life by teaching her how to swear in Hindi. The greatest singers have taught their disciples to sing from the stomach and not the throat, so did Tamanna and Richa – they taught Rihana to swear from the stomach and not the mouth.

Rihana was ecstatic to see them and introduced her best buddies to Veer, who was very warm and welcoming towards his beloved's friends. He even made some small talk about Rihana's laughter and teased her. It all was a merry gathering and Rihana was happy to see Veer taking interest. While exchanging phone numbers with Tamanna and Richa, and asking them in brief about where in Delhi they stayed, he promised to catch up with them in Delhi and moved on to entertain other guests.

Raj attended the ceremony; after all, two of his close friends were getting engaged. Disappointment would have been very obvious with absence. And he chivalrously carried a smile throughout the event. Mostly, he stood in a corner and observed Rihana, her smiles, her frowns, and even her tensed moments before the ceremony.

He walked up to her at the end of the ceremony while she was standing alone, 'Congratulations Rihana! I'm very happy for you.'

Rihana could sense what all was hidden behind that smile, but there wasn't much she could do to console him. She had her own fears gnawing at her. Raj bid goodbye to Rihana and walked out, curtaining his tears behind a pair of Ray Ban aviators. One can probably fake a smile, but how does one mask tears!

Rihana searched her soul to find if she was in any way guilty for his condition. Though she was aware of Raj's feelings for her, she was at wits' end herself. This ceremony had come like a whirlwind and she didn't know what to do. She was sure she wouldn't have caused pain to any living form intentionally, least of all her friend and confidant, Raj.

As it usually is with lovers, Raj's feelings did not die; they just simmered inside his heart. He knew well that one never actually outgrew feelings. So he also learnt how to display appropriate behaviour towards his classmate's fiancée.

The rings were exchanged, the families were happy, the duo was all smiles and it all seemed perfect. Veer left for Delhi shortly thereafter where he was planning to set up his own office. He planned to make Delhi his base with Rihana after marriage for he perceived greater opportunities there.

Forbidden Fruit

Veer left for Delhi, and Rihana was left with her insecurities and fears. A relationship is difficult to manage, and a long distance one with a man who is trying to establish a new venture, breathtakingly difficult.

To counter such negative thoughts, Rihana met Raj, more to ask about Veer than to kindle discomfort, which was anyway inevitable.

'Veer was your classmate in school, Raj. What sort of guy is he?'

Raj replied in a cultured tone, 'Whatever I say about Veer would be perceived as bias, Rihana. He is going to be your husband and it's in your interest to understand him better for having a happy married life with him. My opinion in no way can contribute to the relationship you have to build with him. Even in the future, don't seek opinions; rather make your own. One is the best judge of one's kettle of fish.'

Dumbstruck, Rihana was certain that Raj was concealing something about Veer from her but she did not coerce him to reveal it yet. She knew if there was something in it which could harm her, Raj would never hide it.

Her days rolled in mechanical monotony: she helped her father at work, recharged herself with a swim and Raj's company every evening.

And then one day, when Roop Chand drove her parents out of town for a high-brow social gathering, Caesar, their dog who had not been keeping well for a long time, stopped eating, and then he crashed into a couple of chairs while walking. All didn't seem good to Rihana and she panicked in the absence of everyone she could bank upon if an emergency arose. She called up Veer in a state of panic. The phone rang for more than a couple of minutes and then got disconnected. She could think of just one man then – Raj, her only hope in that predicament. She barely heard the first ring before Raj responded. He could hear Rihana sob.

'Hey Rihana, are you okay?' he asked, upset.

In a quivering voice, she said,'Raj, Caesar is not well. He is not eating and I think has lost his vision too. He needs to be taken to the hospital, but my parents are out of town. I called up the vet and he has asked me to bring Caesar to the clinic without any delay. Will you come with me, please?' asked Rihana. She would have done it all by herself had she not been emotionally snapped.

'I'll be there in ten minutes,' he assured before hanging up.

Raj was outside Rihana's house in no time. After making Caesar comfortable in the back seat of his car, he drove Rihana straight to the veterinary hospital a few miles away. Raj stopped the car in front of the hospital and both of them carried Caesar out of the car. The doctor diagnosed him with Hepatitis and told Rihana that Caesar had lost his sight; that's why he had collided with the chairs too. He gave Caesar a few injections and prescribed some medicines. Raj and Rihana waited till three bottles of glucose were administered to Caesar, after which he gathered some strength.

When they were on their way back with Caesar, Rihana thanked Raj for being of help. Raj feigned anger at being thanked, triggering Rihana's train of thoughts.

'I wish I was your dog!' Raj teased laughingly.

Even in that situation, Raj managed to put a smile on her face.

'Why do you want to be my dog, Raj? And why do you wish to be a dog in the first place?' Rihana sounded relaxed now.

Raj, who always had a lot of tricks up his sleeve, answered smilingly, 'See, I can itch wherever I want to and the public will excuse me. Second, I can express my feeling in public. Third, I will remain with you faithfully.' Raj could discern Rihana's expression change after his third confession. 'Lastly, I won't mind if someone calls me a *kutta*,' Raj concluded hilariously.

Though Rihana laughed at Raj's silly confession, she detested it when anyone called Caesar a *kutta*. She was still thinking what to say to him when her phone rang. It was Veer.

She took the call and without any greetings, Veer rattled off, 'It was a busy day for me. I saw your missed call but could not call back. I had a meeting over lunch and it wouldn't have looked nice to talk in front of everyone. Anyhow, anything important?'

'Just out of concern,' Rihana lied. 'Wanted to know if you are fine. You have been keeping very busy.'

'Yes, I'm okay. What would happen to me,' answered Veer, ignoring the sarcasm.

When Rihana finally told Veer about Caesar not keeping well and her panic, he was withdrawn and didn't offer any succour. She knew he was busy and didn't mind it too much. She was at peace that Caesar was now better.

'Take it to the doctor,' he said unconcernedly in a cold voice.

Rihana said, 'yes' and hung up after a brief 'call you later' from Veer.

Rihana was agitated at Veer's reaction. And after seeing what all Raj had been doing to help her, this sure didn't seem like a good sign. Raj had guessed the exchange but thought it better to stay out of it. After dropping Rihana at her house, he proceeded back to his office.

She settled Caesar and waited for Veer's call. When the phone buzzed, she promptly picked it up in the very first ring, 'Hi Veer!'

'Rihana...' It was Raj.

'I just called up to check that you're not feeding on popcorns and burgers with lots of soft drinks since your mom is away. Remember, eating right is important for girls who are about to get crucified at the altar of marriage. If you become a hog, the gods will enjoy your sacrifice more. You'll give them more blood and flesh. Also, I don't want to take chances with your weight gain!'

Rihana frowned lovingly and burst out in mock anger, 'Why would *you* be taking chances if I put some weight on?'

'What if looking at your bulges, Veer rejects you? Then I'll be forced to marry you,' joked Raj.

'Look at yourself first, you monster,' shouted Rihana and smiled ear to ear.

It had been such silly jokes that had strengthened Rihana's friendship with Raj. He knew what would make her smile, and she savoured the bond to its core.

With the passage of time, Veer's calls reduced to almost none a day. And whenever Rihana expected Veer's call, it would turn out to be Raj's and his one-liner jokes would turn her disappointment into happiness.

On one such day, Rihana was walking back home after a swim. Raj had been late in the office so she was by herself. Just when she was right outside the gate of the huge house, her friend Tamanna, who wasn't keeping well for some time, called her up and said excitedly, 'Hi Rihana! Guess who is with me?' Rihana named a few common friends, but failed to have it right.

Tamanna then handed over the phone to Veer saying, 'Here, talk to your darling.' Rihana was shocked to know that Veer went to Tamanna's house without informing her. Tamanna's acquaintance with Veer was only through Rihana, and moreover, they had met but once on their engagement. Veer merely said, 'I just came to cheer Tamanna up and to wish her the pink of health.' Veer was undoubtedly guilty and that reflected in his tone. Rihana hung up without saying anything and wondered how Veer could find time for her friends when he barely had time to call her up.

She also knew that Tamanna stayed in a rented house with Richa, as their parents were in Bhopal. Richa had also been in the house when Veer went to see them. It must have been troublesome for two girls to host him, especially with a nosy landlady who despised seeing men around the apartments. After Veer left, Tamanna threw a word of caution to Rihana saying, 'Today it was us; tomorrow it can be anyone else. Be careful!'

Veer never had the time to call her, but somehow found time to visit her friends who would never welcome him alone. She wasn't sure if she should feel good about the concern he had for her friend or be upset at his keeping her out of the picture. The words reverberated in her mind, *'Today it was us; tomorrow it can be anyone else. Be careful!'*

Rihana walked into the house in utter confusion, and in that state of mind overheard her parents talking about putting Caesar to rest medically, for he was in great pain and his ailment could not be treated. And they also did not want to tell Rihana about it. When she overheard their discussion, she ran out of the house.

This had been too much to take and she could not think of anyone but Raj.

She literally ran to Raj's house; he was at the door, just about to enter. She went and clung to him crying, 'Raj, they are killing Caesar.' Raj put his arms around her, walked her in and made her sit on his bed, the only piece of furniture, apart from a study table that he had in his room. He sat beside her and hugged her tight. He wiped her tears and held her till she stopped crying. He lifted her face to make her look at him and then spoke in a contained tone, 'Look at me! Rihana, look here.'

As she lifted her face wet with tears and eyes red with pain, he said softly, 'Only two things are not in the hands of a man - marriage and death. They happen when they have to. Caesar is suffering, and putting him to sleep will liberate his soul. Everything in your life has a span. If you stretch it beyond that, it'll only give you pain. Let it go. Let nature act!'

'How can you say that, Raj? They are killing Caesar; how can that be natural?' Rihana protested.

'Yes, it's not natural, but living in excruciating pain is not natural either. Don't see this as harming him. You are ridding Caesar of his pain. Would you be able to see him suffering like this, Rihana?' She looked up at him, eyes shimmering with tears, and she shook her head. It would break her heart to see Caesar suffering in front of her eyes. Raj held her hand and explained, 'It'll make your heart lighter, and Caesar will be at peace!'

After a brief pause, Raj continued, 'You know, my mother died of cancer.' She looked up at him at that instant, her tears and sobs forgotten. Raj had never talked about his mother before this. 'During the last stages, she suffered so much that I prayed and wished every day for her deliverance as I couldn't see her inching towards death. When existence becomes exceedingly painful, death is welcome.'

She dug her face in Raj's arms, his words eased her and she felt relaxed.

'Are you okay?' Raj asked her like a father asks his child.

'And remember, Menaka Gandhi is not listening to our conversation. So your father will not be in jail unless I go and tell her,' Raj said tucking a lone strand of hair behind her ear. Rihana managed a weak smile and thought about Raj's ability to make her smile.

Rihana had already been feeling weak and vulnerable due to Veer's lack of interest in her, and Raj's love wasn't helping. She could sense the intensity of her feelings for Raj increasing, as he was showering her with all the love and attention that she was craving for. She was low on confidence and self-esteem due to Veer's neglect, but it was being taken care of by Raj. Her senses were leaving her body as she nestled in his strong yet tender arms. They were in the perfect situation, with all the ingredients for sparks to fly.

Rihana looked up at Raj, and looked at him long enough to let his eyes penetrate her very being. Her feelings were intense and she burned with desire; yet, she hesitated for a brief second. Raj, reading her dilemma, framed her face tenderly in his hands, and gently kissed her luscious lips. The gentleness was soon taken over by fiery passion with their lips and tongue locked into each other's. The tongues explored and tasted the other, as their senses gave in to the pleasure both were seeking.

The sound of a kiss is not as loud as a cannon's, but its echo lasts a great deal longer. Their bodies were in a state of frenzy and the fire ignited by this passion had to be doused.

Raj began unbuttoning Rihana's red shirt and took it off effortlessly. She was wearing a delicately laced black bra inside, contrasting with her ivory skin, that accentuated his thirst. He tried to unhook her bra but could not quite do it.

'I've never opened one before,' Raj said shyly, albeit panting. Rihana smiled, bent her right arm backwards and undid the hooks for him. He was dazzled to see her assets set free.

'Oh my God! Do you feed these sprightly brats all those burgers and pizzas that I keep asking you to not have?' Raj was gasping for breath as he slowly reached out to hold her.

Rihana punched him lovingly on the back and he sniggered.

Raj lost no time in taking those intoxicating breasts, one by one, in his mouth and nibbled at them. When he freed Rihana of the other stitches on her body, he ran berserk and set out fondling and kissing each bit of her silken body. He was gazing at a woman's splendour in full bloom for the first time, and that too of the ravishingly beautiful Rihana. He was heaving and panting, and to keep his senses on track, kept mumbling 'Oh my God' time and again. Bursting out of his seams, he plunged his face between her thighs and tasted her velvety wetness.

Rihana was in heaven, to say the least. She let go of all her inhibitions and lived each moment of the ecstasy. She was on the verge of a climax when Raj pulled away, leaving her thirsty for more. It was then that Rihana took charge. She unfastened his trousers and boxers and made him lie on the bed. Her eyes were locked with his and there was nothing else that mattered at that time. She mounted him and dexterously rode his bullish monstrosity to manipulate it. Raj was going through the extremes of pleasure, moaning and showering Rihana with pleasurable grunts. Rihana was on top of the world when Raj threw his hands back in a state of ecstasy. Still, to settle the score, he got up and locked his legs around her without untangling himself from her. He delivered her several gratifying thrusts, and she danced hysterically in his lap. She could feel his elephantine hardness strike against the inside of her navel. Their mouths met again and their tongues rolled over each other's, enjoying a state of absolute bliss. For this moment, Rihana had forgotten Caesar and Veer as she had been transported into a world brimming with fulfilment and stillness.

Just when Raj was about to explode, he withdrew himself from Rihana and ejaculated on the bed. He hugged her and they lay there without talking. They could hear each other's heartbeats and let their hearts do the talking.

'I didn't manage to flood your dam, I guess?' Raj asked her, realizing Rihana had not climaxed.

'I don't come the conventional way,' she smiled enigmatically.

'What does that mean?' Raj was curious.

'I need my breasts to be licked and hardened nipples to be pampered, and then I myself have to arouse my clit,' Rihana answered matter-of-factly.

Like a soldier with a command, Raj immediately bent over her and put his tongue to the task. She began moaning, softly at first and then wildly. After a while, she took over her clit and vigorously massaged it till it exploded and she frenzied into an orgasm. She felt better and relaxed. He lay right next to her until she caught a glimpse of the wall clock.

She jumped up realising she would be late. They showered together and quickly dressed up.

While dressing up, she said, 'Next time, if you don't have rubber, we better play carom instead.' By that statement, Raj grew hopeful of many more prospective rendezvous.

Raj offered her dinner, but she declined saying she was full for the night. When he dropped her home, Rihana knew what was in store for her. She walked inside and looked at her mother for the blow to fall.

'Rihana, we took Caesar to the doctor and he breathed his last. We buried him!' She had been straight about it; Rihana believed her. She held back her tears and went to her room, wept till she fell asleep. Nobody in the house ate dinner that night.

The next morning, the house seemed empty without Caesar. Though he had been unwell for long but the knowledge that he would not be seen again just increased everyone's sense of the void that had been created. Rihana came down to the dining table for breakfast to be greeted by her *Nana*, her maternal grandfather. She assumed her mother to have requested him to be present because Rihana shared a special bond with him. Like her Dada, her Nana had been a soldier too, and life never stopped for him. After retiring from the Armed Forces, he had settled in Jaipur with his family and got his daughter, Rihana's mother, married there. Now that her Dada had passed away, the presence of her Nana in that situation was like a streak of sunshine in the darkness, a touch of love amidst hatred. They shared an unusual bonding of love and respect between people who were years apart but had so much to give each other. He got up and took her into his arms.

'Why are you so sad, my love?' Nana asked Rihana.

Rihana's silence was clouded with her own guilt and insecurities. While she was sad about Caesar's demise, she was also engaged to one man and had just slept with another. The grief of losing Caesar was now overtaken by her sense of her culpability. She broke into sobs within no time.

'I'll bring a new pet for you, Rihana. I understand Caesar has gone forever, but the relationship between you and Caesar will always live,' Nana said showing his pragmatism.

Rihana spent time with her Nana the two days that he stayed with them. He told Rihana's mother before leaving that the entire expenditure of Rihana's wedding will be borne by him. He had only stayed that long to make Rihana look beyond death and cherish life.

Raj and Rihana met at the swimming pool two days after Caesar's demise. After swimming, they went to the nearest Café Coffee Day – one of the first to be opened in Jaipur – for a cup of coffee. Raj ordered a simple Cappuccino while Rihana tried a Chocolate Fantasy. Chocolates work wonders on depressed people.

When the sales boy gave the Chocolate Fantasy to Rihana without a spoon, Raj grinned, 'She can have it with her bare hands. But if you give her a spoon, she will look more civilized and will not rub her dirty hands on your new cushions.'

Raj would never miss a chance to rib Rihana.

The sales boy's eyes popped out and he immediately handed over a spoon and a fork to Rihana. She chuckled and walked to a table. Raj followed her. That little conversation at the sales counter broke the silence between them, thanks to the embarrassment of their sudden explosive encounter two days ago.

'Chocolate Fantasy has four hundred calories,' said Raj with a titter. 'You are very close to rejection.'

'Do you ever take anything seriously?' said Rihana.

'Okay, that serious question again – what do you feed them with?' Raj said eyeing her ample breasts, a mischievous smile playing on his lips.

'Stop it, Raj!' Rihana landed a loving blow on his arm.

'No, seriously, I mean they are abundant,' exclaimed Raj.

When Rihana did not look up and dug into her Chocolate Fantasy instead, Raj said casually, 'I love your dog, you know. After his death, I've developed a special attachment with him. May God bless his soul,' prayed Raj.

Rihana could sometimes not judge whether Raj was serious or not. Exasperated with his jokes on Caesar's death and his obsession with her anatomy, she started crying.

Raj felt sorry for his idiosyncrasies and apologized. He then offered her a tissue paper and waited till she calmed down. But when was he the one to remain silent. So after a while, he muttered,

'By the way, you plundered my virginity.'

Rihana forgot her anger and pain and blurted at a higher volume than she would have otherwise,'What! Don't tell me that you were...,' she shook her head and again continued, '...Were you a virgin at twenty-five?'

'Yes I was, and I am blessed to have lost my virginity to a nymph like you. You made it worth losing.' And then, suddenly striking a sober note he said, 'Whatever has happened is done. Don't carry the burden, for some events are inevitable. No matter how much we try to control the situation, sometimes losing control is the best option. But tell me, how are you so good at this art of love-making?'

Rihana answered spiritedly, 'I have a big collection of porn. All my desires and fantasies have been fuelled from there. Believe it or not, that was my first time too. I picked up everything that I know, that you seemed to love, from there,' she answered sheepishly.

'Porn!' screamed Raj.

'Stop shouting! And why are you men such hypocrites? Why can't you accept women as individuals having their exclusive needs? Men behave as if they monopolize the three letter word: SEX. Every man has a cache of porn either on his laptop or mobile, but if it's with a girl, it becomes a taboo. A man wants his woman to do everything that is done in porn, but does not want her to watch it. How will she ever discover what her man wants if she does not know it herself? And you ought to understand that pornography is the major driving force behind excessive internet usage; more than seventy percent of internet usage is related to pornography. It's a simple rule of demand and supply. Let me also tell you that no one has been hanged so far for watching porn. Huh! Why in the world did you give such a strange, over-the-top reaction?' asked Rihana.

Raj went quiet following Rihana's aggression, but then after a pause, spoke very softly, 'As a matter of fact, I don't watch porn myself unless it becomes a want. I know porn is a necessary evil, but it numbs people towards sexual violence. It also makes a person desensitized to sexual arousal which leads to delayed orgasm, a blessing in disguise – the one you experienced in my company. Is porn the best way to know what a man wants from a woman?'

'It could be a good way to know what a man wants from a woman, but definitely not the best way to know what a woman wants from a man. Porn is also very men-centric.' She paused for a moment and continued, 'You don't watch porn and you were a virgin till two days back? Did some sex guru give you personal lessons and dish out this gyaan to you?' Rihana had a dig at Raj, not missing the rare chance.

'Google guru, sweetheart!' blurted Raj. He took a deep breath and continued, 'You've watched porn to the extent that you've got used to your own fingers; it's become a habit for you. A man derives immense pleasure in serving his partner's needs. Aren't you depriving your man of that joy? Self-dependence is good, but not when others can take care of it. Lovemaking is a mutual process and each partner deserves his or her share of ensuing bliss,' insisted Raj.

'Stop being judgmental, Raj. Using my fingers doesn't mean that I don't need a partner or don't get aroused by his touch. It's just that I know my body well and I know clearly and precisely where to tickle myself,' Rihana was brutally assertive.

Raj bent forward on the table to come close to Rihana and said flirtingly, 'Sweetie, give me a chance and I promise you'll never regret it.'

Their blue conversation came to an abrupt halt when Rihana's mobile buzzed and her display read, 'Headquarter calling'. Headquarter was an alias for her mother – the only person Rihana dreaded and respected with equal intensity.

Raj cleared the bill like every time while she hurriedly wrapped up her grub and headed home.

At home, her mother was furious. 'Where the hell were you?' She enquired tersely.

Rihana, not used to lying, told her that she was with Raj. Her mother became all the more agitated and ordered, 'You'll not go out with anyone from now onwards. You've to understand that in a few months, you'll be married. These few months are the most crucial; nothing should go wrong. I don't want anyone talking about my daughter, especially when she is about to get married into such an influential family.'

After a few minutes of talking at a high pitch and Rihana's silence, she mellowed down and resumed her talk, 'Baby, the world is a hostile place for women. You need to understand the complications involved with these little deeds of yours. Things can get blown into a full time scandal that can completely tarnish your image and seal your future. We're guilty of many lapses in our lives, but not the ones that destroy us completely.'

Rihana felt like the post-interval Simran of *DDLJ* with Raj running amok in her thoughts. The turmoil going on in her mind had a different road that led her to a different address. Her physical intimacy with Raj had brought her even closer to him and it worried her immensely. Feelings of guilt, insecurity and confusion had engulfed her so much that she wasn't able to differentiate between right and wrong. She was getting carried away by Raj's want and love for her that was not at all evident in Veer's interactions with her, howsoever much they were.

Summers had given way to a mild nip in the air, which among other things, signalled the approach of the Hindu festive season and Rihana's birthday. She was born on the day of Diwali, and her mother celebrated her birthday on that day, irrespective of the date Diwali fell on. It was a day of celebration of the return of Lord Rama to his kingdom after defeating the wicked Ravana. So, like every other year, there was a grand party on the eve of Diwali at the Gymkhana Club and it was attended by all the members and influential families across Jaipur. Rihana was decked up in a white *churidaar* and *kurti* with a multi-coloured *lehriya dupatta*, Jaipur's specialty. She wore matching colourful bangles on the right wrist while a luxury watch studded with diamonds rested on the left. She stuck a bindi on her forehead fondly remembering her Dada. She looked ravishingly beautiful in that attire. Her mother was dressed in a resplendent red sari with a thin golden border. She looked very young for her age and was quite a sensation. Who was more irresistible? The choice was befuddling. Everyone in the huge, well-lit, decorated hall envied Veer, for he had both in his family now – one as his wife and the other as his mother-in-law.

Rihana had told Raj about her conversation with her mother the moment she had closed the door of her room behind her the same day and he chose not to embarrass the family by meeting Rihana in public. He called Rihana up on her phone, but she was lost in the music on the dance floor. She was dancing with her father because of the strict instructions given by her mother to not dance with anyone other than him or Veer. Rihana could dance even to the vibrating sound of a generator; the music that day was a treat. She wanted to leave behind all her worries and dance. Dancing to the tunes she loved always acted as a stress-buster; it gave her a high that no drug in the world could probably match.

While dancing, she felt her mobile buzz in the little pouch she carried. She dug her phone out and saw 'Raj calling' displayed on the screen. She went off the floor to attend the call. Raj did not want to wish her on the wrong date and insisted to do that a few days later, the actual date of her birth. But on call, he asked her to sneak out of the party and come to the room adjoining the party hall. She was petrified and had her mental reservations to the idea. She wasn't sure of the purpose behind Raj calling her to the room; but the feelings of doubt were overpowered by the feelings of faith, anticipation and excitement. After a moment of scepticism, she finally decided to take the plunge.

She looked around the hall, acting as if the signal was weak and the sound of music was making it impossible for her to hear the one on the other end of the line, and walked out of the hall on that pretext. When Rihana quietly slipped through the open door of the room a few steps away, she saw Raj sitting on the armrest of the couch, holding a basket that had a small Labrador pup in it. He had tied a ribbon around the pup's neck holding a tag that read, "Happy birthday to the girl who looted my virginity."

She ran to him, hugged him and kissed him passionately. Once again, the situation was getting out of control, for their bodies craved for each other. But Raj quickly came to his senses. He disengaged himself from the kiss to make sure her birthday celebrations were not marked with anything that would be regretted by both later.

'Control, my dear girl, or else I'll be doubly fucked by your hot mom and *khadoos baap*,' Rihana shot him a disgusted look and punched him playfully, to which he added, 'By the way, how could your mom marry him? I'm always at sixes and sevens at this thought,' teased Raj.

'If I get married to you, people will say the same thing – round peg in a square hole,' retorted Rihana in defence of her father.

'But I'm not an ass like your dad. Now, before I become a victim of this situation, let's return to the party,' whispered Raj.

'What should I do with this present?' entreated a bewildered Rihana.

'I'll have someone drop it to your house. Don't worry!' assured Raj. 'And I will remove the tag too,' he winked.

He gave her a quick peck and she went back to the party. Rihana's mother was not aware of this little escape, but the few waiters who had seen her go out and then return with Raj informed her father. Raj was right – he had become the victim. Rihana's parents were waiting up for her after the party and she was expecting her birthday to end with a fireworks display. And there were fireworks alright, but of a kind that Rihana had not expected from her parents.

She was met with an eerie, angry, stony silence from her parents. Both were sitting with their arms crossed, glaring at her. She knew it was futile to ignore their expression, so she sat down beside them with a sigh. Her father spoke first, 'Rihana, I've never opposed anything that you have done. But today was the biggest disappointment of my life. I'm not sure if I'm more angry or ashamed. What have you done?'

His face was flushed with anger and he continued with even more anger in his tone, 'And this, in spite of your mother telling you about all the pitfalls of hanging out with a scoundrel, that too after your engagement?' Rihana wanted to protest. Her heart and body were still singing from having just met Raj. But one look at her parents, and she knew she would put Raj into more trouble than he already was in. It would infuriate her parents further. Though Rihana's parents knew Raj and his association with their daughter, they had just become overprotective. They didn't want anything to go wrong before the marriage. Rihana listened to everything her parents had to say and made up her mind that her meetings with Raj would have to be more clandestine.

The repercussions for Raj were quite serious. Her father decided to meet Raj the very next day. He went to Raj's office and within a closed cabin, threatened him with dire consequences if he did not keep his hands off his daughter. The staff members at Raj's office witnessed this meeting, though they could not hear what passed between the men. Raj was perplexed with the questioning looks everyone shot at him.

Moreover, in a city like Jaipur, an incident such as this could have the gossip mills running for at least a month. No wonder Raj had called Rihana's father an ass. Any sensible father would make his daughter understand instead of threatening her boyfriend. And Raj also wondered how this man was as successful as he was in business and yet, could not see that by berating him in public, he was also making his daughter a subject of gossip in the public gaze!

The Vows and Woes

Veer flew down from Delhi to Jaipur for Rihana's birthday, which by date was a few days after Diwali. He took a morning flight from Delhi and was excited to meet Rihana when he landed in mid-afternoon. Rihana, this time, did not share the same enthusiasm. Her mind and heart were stuck on her affection for Raj and the fact that Veer had time for everyone but her didn't help much.

He brought her a birthday present, and her parents gave excited and happy reactions to that. She received the gift with noticeable disinterest and earned for herself a dirty look from her mother. Her mother prodded her to open the gift, joking with Veer if it was something too personal to be seen in front of them. Veer laughed out and cleared that it was safe to open it.

Rihana was least excited about Veer, but she had always liked gifts. So, curious about the gift he had brought, she unwrapped it as her parents watched her do so. It was a photo frame with a picture of Veer standing beside his Audi R8.

Rihana sighed, showing the present to her mother. She saw the look on her mother's face and the expectant smile on Veer's, and thought it best to take the safest bet.

'As insipid as your would be son-in-law, mom,' she handed over the photo frame to her mother and walked out of the room on the pretext of feeding Tiger, a prized possession bestowed upon her by someone who really loved her. It was the first time that Rihana realized that love, like yawning, is contagious. She was beginning to get infected with that virus.

Rihana was quiet all through as Veer sat with her parents over lunch and then got up to go, see his own parents. Rihana went with him to see him off and while he was trying to be close to her, she was uneasy in his presence and with his touch.

To her, Veer's coming to see her and her family before meeting his parents was also somewhat strange. For all she knew, he could have been excited to meet her. But his behaviour otherwise didn't fit into that assumption. Moreover, according to her, it was only appropriate to adhere to protocol. She expected him to see his parents first. She got along with Veer's parents pretty well; they were simple, 'no-frills-attached' people. Though Veer's parents were very fond of her, she was undoubtedly closer to Veer's father.

After Veer left, Rihana's mother came up to her to ask her about her behaviour towards Veer but she dismissed the queries and spent the evening in her room, with Tiger and the memories of the one she thought she had fallen in love with. The same evening, Veer took Rihana and a few of their friends for dinner. Veer invited Raj too, giving Rihana a strong alibi if her parents came to know about it. Raj resisted, but Rihana forced him to join them. Raj had understood well what trouble his closeness to Rihana could create for him, so he kept to himself. His interactions during the dinner were restricted. That's because when you speak less, the probability of saying wrong things also reduces.

'Rihana, you look dazzling today,' said Ravi Poonia who had accompanied Veer to Thailand too. Rihana assumed it to be a genuine compliment and thanked him with a smile.

'I like the fragrance you are wearing. Which one is it?' asked Ravi.

'Thanks, it's Bvlgari White. My aunt picked it up for me,' replied Rihana.

'How was your Thailand trip then? All alone...,' Ravi kept the conversation going.

She smiled as the memories of a wonderful holiday came rushing to her mind, 'I really enjoyed myself. I tried my hands on as many adventure sports as I could. That's what I had gone there for in the first place,' replied Rihana.

'Oh, really? Usually people go to Thailand for something else," he smirked, but there was silence as nobody else spoke. In fact, everyone at the table who was till now involved in some conversation or the other stopped short and paid attention to Ravi and Rihana. Ravi took a quick look at Veer's face and covered up by asking her, 'Do you travel alone all the time or was this a special occasion?'

Rihana had been so used to this question by everyone now that she answered exasperated, 'All my friends backed out at the last moment and I didn't want to keep something that I really wanted to do pending, just for the lack of company.'

'You should definitely not restrict yourself and must pack your bags often to see as much of the world as possible. My job doesn't give me enough chances, or else I would have mapped the whole world by now. When you travel to new places, your world and opinions change,' exhorted Ravi.

Rihana's world was anyway going to change in a few months, she thought. The families were only waiting for Veer's sister to return from a pleasure trip so she could attend the wedding ceremony, binding them for life.

Engulfed in her thoughts, Rihana was shaken by a voice, 'Veer, you're lucky to get such a wife –beautiful and cultured. The combination that Rihana displays is indeed rare,' complimented Ravi.

Rihana beamed at the compliment and thanked him earnestly. Raj's presence on the table and his ignoring her wasn't doing her any good. So, this compliment came as a welcome change and reminder of her awaiting fate at the same time.

They ordered several dishes from the Indian cuisine, and everyone at the table made decorous use of cutlery to eat their food. Veer, on the other hand, preferred the cutlery nature has bestowed everyone with. His plate was heaped with food and he dug his hands into it with full gusto. It amazed Rihana because she was a very small eater herself. Thanks to her grandfather's stories, she held a belief that people who ate more in the early years of their lives died of starvation in the later years. Not just the story, she knew well that on the health front, making a pig out of oneself would put one's life in danger.

Looking at him hogging like that, digging into a plate heaped with food with his bare hands, she had already started resenting Veer's eating habits. The dinner ended with a dessert but Veer's loud burp and laughter thereafter sapped all sweetness out of Rihana's sweet dish.

While it was time to bid goodbyes, Raj was aloof and made sure to keep away from Rihana and Veer. Just then, Veer threw a nasty comment at Ravi, 'Keep the compliments reserved for your mother, you nincompoop. You have been showering my fiancée with compliments ever since the evening started. Looks to me like you have the hots for her!'

Rihana saw Ravi's face turn red and then pink with embarrassment and anger, respectively. Soon after Veer said that, his face masked that evil temper from a moment ago and he feigned social pleasantries, 'Good night friends, and thank you for coming.'

He then held Rihana's hand and pulled her into the car. She saw him seething with rage and burning with jealousy, the reasons for which Rihana could not understand. He drove the car at breakneck speed, which made Rihana tremble.

'You're *not* going to talk to Ravi after this. Ever. Do you understand that?' Veer shouted.

Nobody had ever talked to Rihana in a raised voice, and here was a guy who she was supposed to get married to, shouting at her. She went numb for a few moments. She just wanted to reach home and rid herself from the clutches of this angry monster. The moment the car stopped in front of her house, she jumped out and rushed in without a word to Veer.

She was crying hysterically when she entered and saw her grandmother sitting in the living room. She ran straight into her arms.

'What happened?' asked her Dadi, confused and taken aback at her tears.

'Dadi, I don't want to marry Veer. He behaves like an animal from a different planet. I don't know what's wrong with him...but I don't want to marry him,' cried Rihana.

She then narrated the whole incident to her Dadi, who listened to her with rapt attention and sympathy. Women of her age had far more insight into the behaviour of men because they had seen them in myriad relationships.

It was not much later that Rihana's parents came rushing to the living room; Rihana's cries were loud enough to have woken up the entire city. Rihana ran into her mother's arms next and repeatedly stressed that Veer wasn't a good choice. She let her emotions loose that day and told her family how Veer had not bothered to call her since the engagement or pay any attention to her. And yet, he ticked off a perfect gentleman's compliments by objectifying her and treating her like she was already his property. Her parents listened patiently, but soon termed the incident as merely an excuse to shun Veer; they were aware of her feelings for Raj.

'If she doesn't want to marry the boy, why are you forcing her?' interfered her grandmother. She knew too well what forcing a marriage on someone could do to their spirit. 'I want Rihana to be happy; I don't care about people and what they say. If her happiness doesn't lie in this marriage, call it off!' advised an over-indulgent but worldly-wise Dadi.

'But Mummyji, the entire fraternity knows about the engagement. How can we ignore what they say? She should have taken this decision earlier. All women have to adjust and make compromises. Haven't we done it?' Rihana's mother looked at Rihana and her Dadi by turns. 'You and I have gone through the same horrors of a marriage, maybe worse than what she is crying over. She is saying all this because of that Raj who looks like a junglee. She doesn't realize that she will end up with children who look like zebras. Don't we have to think about our future generations? That boy has corrupted her mind,' said Rihana's agitated mother.

'Preeti!' This one word silenced Rihana's mother and made Rihana take comfort in her Dadi's lap once more. 'Are you bothered about what people say more than your daughter? Haven't we women suffered enough with these monkeys that you're bothered about a junglee in the family? We will tame the junglee also. And if you know she likes some other boy, why don't you get her married to him? What's the harm?' She ran her hand over Rihana's head in her lap and lovingly added, 'And I will appreciate if you stop being a racist and call that boy by his name.'

Rihana was thankful to god for her Dadi's presence; she knew not how she could have managed her parents single-handedly, amidst sobs.

'Mummyji, what is the guarantee that she will be happy with Raj after we get her married to him? Ugly husbands are insecure too, especially when they have good-looking wives. I want a better life for my daughter and I'm equally concerned,' said Rihana's mother with finality.

⚘

Bothered by her daughter's tears and confused at her mother-in-law's warning, Rihana's mother called Veer up. He was on his way to the airport to catch a flight for Delhi, but clarity on this issue was of prime importance.

'Veer, what did you do to Rihana last night that she is refusing to marry you?' asked Rihana's mother sternly.

'Nothing Mummy, we just had dinner with our friends and I dropped her home,' Veer said meekly.

'You will have to come here and sort this issue out at the earliest...for your own good,' commanded Rihana's mother. Veer was given no option but to make amends. He dropped the idea of going to Delhi but instead headed straight to Rihana's house to meet her and her parents. Rihana did not speak to anyone after the heated argument at home. She was tempted to call up Raj but decided against it because she did not wish him to be blamed for that unsavoury situation. But since she was adamant about not getting married to Veer, her parents were in turmoil and waited for the situation to ease down.

A dead-air prevailed in the house until Veer arrived. When Veer walked into the house, there was an awkward silence. After some cajoling, Rihana joined them in the drawing room, though on the condition that she was not to be left alone with Veer at any time. She figured that if he was really man enough, he would not mind facing her and her family together.

Veer tried to talk in his best tone, 'Rihana, may I know your reason for calling off this wedding? What went wrong? I sincerely wish you give me a chance to explain whatever you took objection to.'

'I don't think I can fiddle with you. We're playing different strings,' said Rihana firmly.

Rihana's father interrupted this conversation that was going nowhere and said, 'Rihana, to be fair to Veer, you need to explain your objections'.

Rihana broached the incident involving Ravi Poonia at the party and told him that his anger, ill-temper and seeming jealousy terrified her. She repeated what she had already told her parents, that his anger against both her and Ravi after the incident was misplaced and stank of a lack of respect for all concerned. All this while, Veer had been staring hard at her, and just to show him that she knew what she was doing, Rihana stared right back and said decisively, 'My decision is final; I will not marry you.'

Veer played the defensive tactic for a while, 'Rihana, you are my fiancée, and you don't know what men are like. That Ravi was complimenting you, or so you seem to imagine, but inside, I know he had lecherous intentions. You are not familiar with the ways of the world. You are a babe in the woods…' He continued, but none of it seemed convincing enough a reason to Rihana.

He then, like a chameleon, changed colour. Not seeing defence working, he veered around and used the sympathy card, which he knew would work to a great extent.

'Rihana, I was just trying to save you and keep Ravi in his right place so that he doesn't bother you when I am not around. I am just possessive about you, and if you don't like that, I promise I will try to work on it.' Rihana looked up at him, wondering whether this was coming from his clear conscience or a scheming businessman's mind.

'Please don't do this to me and my family, Rihana. My father suffered a heart attack a few months back. He is so fond of you; he will be devastated with this decision,' pleaded Veer. There was a complete reversal of character: from a roaring lion to a spineless lamb. She was amazed to see how two contradicting dispositions lay dormant in the same person.

'I can't afford to lose my father. He is very attached to you and adores you.' Rihana's eyes watered; she was genuinely fond of his father. She presumed him to be patient, loving and rich with experience, just like her Nana. Seeing her melt, Veer became sure that he had caught her at her Achilles' heel.

She gave in, and let Veer take over.

♀

A day had passed after this rendezvous and Veer seemed to have taken a few remedial measures. He called her up twice every day, albeit for a few seconds only and more like a dose of medicine to be taken. Rihana made peace with it, hoping that things would get better and smooth with time.

The next day, her friend Tamanna called her and told her that she will be visiting Jaipur soon. Rihana was ecstatic, for she was craving good company and really wanted to ease her heart with someone she could trust. Tamanna told her of a club in Jaipur hosting Enrique, the well-known Spanish singer. She wanted some help from Veer to arrange the passes. She knew that Veer had contacts and it was easier for him to get the passes; plus, the club was owned by one of his friends. On Tamanna's request, she reluctantly called Veer up. The mobile rang for almost a minute before he picked up.

'Hello...' A disinterested voice said on the other end.

The tone grated on Rihana as she had just done Veer a favour by reconsidering the decision. And now, her ego was making her think over the decision of asking for a favour from Veer. At the same time, she did not want to let down her best friend Tamanna. After all, what does one live for – friends and family. That was the only thought that spurred her to call Veer while he was still in Jaipur.

'Veer, I wanted to know if you can arrange for two passes for my friends for Enrique's show in Jaipur? In the same club that your friend owns,' asked Rihana.

'I'm slightly busy right now. I will check and call you in the evening,' answered Veer.

With cordial goodbyes, they hung up. Rihana waited till late in the evening, but Veer didn't call. So she called Tamanna up and told her that Veer would try and that nothing was confirmed yet. Tamanna could sense some hesitation in Rihana's voice and asked her the reason for it. There was so much she wanted to say, but kept it to herself.

Veer called the next day, 'Hi Rihana! I'm leaving for Delhi today evening. Our families have been working on taking dates out for the marriage ceremony and I will let you know the same as soon as possible,' said Veer. William Shakespeare was right when he said, 'Time goes on crutches till love hath all his rites.' Now, after her denial once, Veer was impatient to get married and have Rihana at his side. And overnight, he had completely forgotten about Rihana's request.

She thought that it was futile to remind him, and instead gathered up her courage and dialled Raj.

'Hi! Hope I am not disturbing you? Are you busy?' asked Rihana as she could hear a lot of humdrum behind him.

'No *yaar*! I am never busy for you. Tell me, what happened?' Raj asked casually.

'I need two passes for Enrique's show,' said Rihana.

'That shouldn't be tough. I'll make arrangements,' assured Raj.

It wasn't about the arrangement of passes anymore; suddenly it had become a test for Rihana to fathom the depth of a man's feelings for her.

Rihana went through two extremes – the heights of ecstasy because of Raj and the bottom of despondency because of Veer – at the same time, and was unable to differentiate. Sometimes things don't make sense immediately. It is over a period of time that one starts differentiating between shades. Understanding people and emotions clearly was a tough task. Every individual is an amalgam of different emotions and the way they erupt in different situations. That way, people's habits, whether good or bad, are often mirrors to help someone predict their natures.

Rihana was yet to find out if Veer's aggressive, boorish and inurbane personality was a mere eruption of emotions, or if it was a habit. If they were habits, Rihana was in a fix.

☿

'When your heart persistently says "No", how can your tongue say "Yes"? I'm in a fix, Raj. I want to be out of this situation. I've spoken to Bua, told her everything between you and me. She has suggested we run away. Parents accept everything later; I am sure mine will too. Please let's elope,' Rihana blurted out with utter desperation.

It was a pleasant Saturday afternoon and she had told her mother that she wanted to go check some new designs out for her wedding attire, but had landed up at Raj's place instead. She was already in tears when he opened the door for her, and not much had changed in the past few minutes.

Raj held her face in his hands and looked into her eyes moist with emotions, 'I know you very well, Rihana. You can never do this and be a cause of pain to so many people. You're not capable of putting everyone's happiness at stake like this. Will you ever be able to forgive yourself if something happens to Veer's father after this decision? Forget his father, what about your parents? You're not that selfish; I know you.'

Rihana stared at him in confusion. She could not fathom if he was trying to convince *her,* or *himself.* She couldn't even make out whether all that he had just said about her was true. She was in a quandary to differentiate whether all that he said were questions or answers. It was the first time she wasn't sure whether he was going to stand by her. Was he hesitating to take that step, she wondered. Confusion is a dangerous option out of a critical problem; Rihana was dwelling amidst just that.

Raj had said all this to Rihana very confidently, but inside his heart and mind, there was a storm of unimaginable proportion. It was rooting his reason out and tossing his feelings. He felt strongly in favour of what Rihana had just been suggesting, but his behaviour was not in congruence to his feelings. Was he escaping commitment that Rihana wanted the most? Just for a happy and convenient today, he was pushing the love of his life into suffering in the future?

Or like most men, he also had accomplished his mission of sleeping with a girl and now was running away from commitment. Maybe he had bigger plans than marrying Rihana? She couldn't find the answer immediately.

Rihana freed herself from Raj and he made no attempt to stop her. He was confused, yes, but Rihana knew she would have to live with the truth for the rest of her life that Raj did not take a stand with her when she needed it the most.

Rihana reached home to find her family celebrating the announcement of the date of marriage – fourteenth of February, Valentine's Day, the day of lovers. The smile that marked the irony of the date was perceived by her parents as that of happiness, and she made no efforts to explain. Maybe Raj was right, maybe she could not make so many people unhappy as against just one, herself.

Rihana's mother hugged her as she joined them and said in a contained tone, 'Rihana, I vouch for Veer, my dear. If there's any day that you aren't happy with him or things go beyond your endurance, you come right back to us, your family. We will always be by your side.' Rihana looked at her and desperately wanted to believe in her mother's faith in Veer. 'Be happy now, you're getting married. This is a very special day in every girl's life and you should enjoy every bit of it. Don't ruin it with thoughts of future insecurities. May God bless you,' her mother tried to pep her up.

Listening to her mother, Rihana couldn't help but think that this was not quite the usual mother-daughter pre-wedding speech.

The essence of her mother's words seemed to suggest that she was the sacrificial lamb to keep the honour of the family intact. Her mother was offering her backup plans to return home, even before the marriage had happened.

♂

Rihana was the eldest amongst all her cousins, all of them boys. Being the only daughter of the house, the marriage had to be undoubtedly grand. She was treated like a princess, and none of her demands were ignored. It made her feel as if they were covering up for that one wish that was denied to her – of a life partner of her choice.

Punjabi marriage celebrations generally last for a week, and relatives and friends had gathered from all over the country for this one too. Celebration was in the air as everyone seemed in a jovial mood. Punjabi weddings are also a kind of status symbol: the more ostentatious the wedding, the higher your stand in society. Though Veer and his family were Rajputs, they had no objections to celebrations in the Punjabi way. One could see the amalgamation of both the cultures during the wedding with equal respect and harmony.

Seeing the happiness on the faces of her family members and friends, and the festive mood that prevailed in the house almost all day long, Rihana forgot her worries about Veer. Moreover, Raj's not being able to make up his mind for her had made her confidence take a downward leap. She had decided to not be in touch with him from now on. So now, even if not by choice, she was enjoying her wedding and all the attention she was showered with. Her mother had been right, it seemed - those were the best four days of her life. She talked, danced, gossiped, loved and laughed.

On the D-day, as she recited the vows while marrying Veer, she also made a bigger promise to herself – to make her marriage work.

The toughest and most painful part of the marriage was her farewell from the house where she had spent every moment of her life, to which she belonged. She had been a pampered child, but she was sure that the pain she experienced then was far more excruciating than any other. After she had hugged everyone goodbye, she saw Roop Chand standing in one corner. He was crying more than her parents, and that filled her eyes with tears of insecurities. Everyone in this house – starting from her parents and both sets of grandparents, even Roop Chand – had given her immense love. She felt diffident about her life ahead, that too with a man who didn't understand her. Now stepping out of her parent's house, she had no other choice but to have faith and keep hope to change things for the better, not aware of the naked truth that it was not that easy to change people.

Rihana was accorded a warm welcome into the new family by her in-laws, especially her father-in-law. A happy-go-lucky but a saintly man, he had forsaken the entire ancestral property to his only younger brother and worked his way up for himself. When Rihana once asked him the reason for that, he had said, 'Matters of land are tricky in villages. If you get into them, you're not sure if you'll even get a piece of it to be buried under.' He was ecstatic to have found a daughter like Rihana.

Veer's sister Priyanka left for her husband's house in Jodhpur with him the next evening. That left Rihana in the new house with her new immediate family. It was dinner time when Veer's mother asked him to fetch some ice-cream from the market nearby and asked him to take Rihana along. On their way to the market, Rihana saw her house race past in the car window and felt heavy in her heart. When Veer found her looking longingly at her house, he offered, 'Would you want to spend some time with your parents till I'm in the market?'

Rihana's face beamed with joy and she agreed readily.

More than the pleasure of being with her people, she was happy with Veer's empathy. Her hopes of bonding with him grew stronger.

When Rihana entered the gate of her house, the first one to greet her was Tiger. All others must have seen Tiger running out, so they followed. She hugged her Dadi and cried. They were happy to see her, but also thought that it was inappropriate for her to have come without informing her in-laws. She shared a quick bite with them as the dinner was laid. In the meantime, Veer had come back to pick her up and joined them on the table. He ate a full meal after a full meal.

They bade goodbye and reached Veer's house. Rihana was visibly relaxed and Veer also looked happy at her happiness. His mother teased them that they had taken that long for getting ice cream, which now seemed more like milk shake, thanks to the heat. But this little chit chat apart, both of them were ushered into Veer's room.

As soon as Veer entered and bolted the door behind his back, his penetrating glance made Rihana hopeful about his feelings for her. He was eyeing her lovingly, with a mysterious smile playing on his lips, making her feel that he was up to something. She dashed into the bathroom and changed into a night dress. Now with all her make-up and heavy clothes gone, she felt much more comfortable. But her ivory bangles were vexatious. Although as per Punjabi traditions, a newly-wed bride wears red and white bangles, Rihana had to wear ivory bangles as a Rajput tradition. She didn't have any reservations to this as the red and white bangles would have irritated her just as much.

What followed was a fast-forward version of a moment that every girl waits for. Veer was clumsy with his efforts in consummating their marriage. But that also made Rihana believe that he had not been with many women. And that thought was definitely comforting to her. He undressed her hurriedly, and while gazing at her bare beauty, got very impatient. There were no warm ups and he entered Rihana in haste. She was as dry as the desert of Jaipur and that made his entry violent, which led to drastic consequences. Rihana screamed in pain, followed by bleeding due to vaginal abrasion. Veer took to his side of the bed when he was relieved and Rihana was left in pain. Rihana's mind and body were not in coordination; nor did Veer make an attempt to help her. He was brash.

The next morning, she walked like a duck whose legs were tied. That made her mother-in-law enquire into the reason for her awkward gait. When she told her that she was hurting in her private parts, she was promptly taken to a doctor. On the way to the hospital, Veer's mother commanded, 'Veer, you must go slow,' to which Veer nodded in affirmation. Veer was equally, if not more, embarrassed at this statement.

The gynaecologist examined Rihana and suggested abstinence from sexual intercourse till the healing, and prescribed a few ointments.

The evidence of Rihana's lacerated vagina was undeniable and yet again proved Veer's callous attitude. Rihana still kept hope to differentiate his habits from character. She was hoping to reverse his habits for their happiness. Whenever any thoughts about Raj crossed her mind, she brushed them off by reminding herself of the vows she had taken during the marriage.

After a week or so, Veer and Rihana left for Delhi to settle in their new house. Veer had set up his office and bought a house in Delhi much before the marriage was solemnized. Rihana left Tiger behind with her mother as she did not want anything that would remind her of Raj. One has to give up on one's past for a better tomorrow.

She desperately hoped for things to be simplified.

The Unexpected Welcome

The newly-weds decided to drive down to Delhi in their new car, a sparkling Mercedes ML-350 gifted to Rihana by her mother. Rihana was literally shifting out of the city and had a whole lot of luggage to be taken with her. Her mother had taken such great care of everything for her daughter's comfort – more so in the light of certain recent events – that even before Rihana could start worrying about settling down in a new city, all arrangements had been taken good care of. Household items like refrigerator, air conditioners, washing machine, etc., were delivered to Delhi much before the wedding. Veer's parents were not at all demanding like most of the other boy's parents, so dowry was out of question. But Rihana's mother had collected small little things, and many bigger things, for her marriage since Rihana was a small kid. She had waited for this day ever since and today she was very happy to bestow Rihana with all those gifts. The collection varied from Swarovski crystals, Pashmina shawls, silk saris to solitaires. Most of the stuff had been sent with the household items beforehand, but her mother had suggested that she carries the expensive jewellery with them in the car.

Rihana was hoping that the four hour drive would give her some time alone with Veer, without anything else on his mind. But Veer was mostly quiet on the pretext that he was getting distracted, or talking over phone about his work. Rihana made peace with it and dozed off for a while. They had to enter Delhi through Gurgaon, which is a bustling region with numerous high-rise buildings, so Veer suggested stopping for coffee at a small joint right before that.

Veer finally stopped the car in front of a small cafe on the highway and asked Rihana to wait in the car while he checked if they had something to eat as well. Just when he was about to enter, the door opened and two men came towards Veer and grabbed him. Rihana rushed out of the car, but her shriek was muffled midway by sturdy hands of two men right behind her. Two of the four men pushed Veer and Rihana in the back seat, all four of them squeezing in; while two others took front seat and the wheel.

Rihana was new to the area but she could see deserted pathways all around the car; the goons must be taking them to a secluded place. She used the better of her wisdom and did not protest. All the men in the car were armed and since Veer was trying to retaliate, one of them hit Veer on the head. He fainted with the impact. Rihana was horrified; a million thoughts came running to her mind. Tears were streaming down her cheeks when her hands were tied behind her back and she was blindfolded. She was in a state of panic and said fervent prayers to all the thirty-three crore gods she had heard existed in the Hindu pantheon.

Her prayers fell silent when she heard the four men discussing in a thick Bihari accent whether a ransom was to be collected for the young girl too or if they should sell her to an agent from Nepal for prostitution. Rihana was terrified to begin with, visuals of her impending fate flashing in her mind to accentuate her trouble. Her fear soon took form of anger for Veer; he should be bringing forth his Rajput valour *now* to combat the situation they were stuck in. But he was foolish enough to protest against armed men, four of them, and now lay unconscious in the back seat while the goons planned to sell off his wife.

She was trying to think of a way out when the man behind the wheel stopped the car abruptly. She was squeezed in awkwardly and hit her head on the back of the seat ahead of her as the car stopped. Just then she heard one of the men say in crude Bihari, 'Just check if that man is still alive!'

Rihana hadn't imagined it could be that bad, and freaked out completely. Hearing her scream, they stuffed her mouth with a cloth. It tasted horrible, but more because of the feeling that something might have happened to Veer. She was now genuinely worried for Veer; all said and done, he was her husband now.

All her sensory organs were blocked, except for her ears, so she listened. The four men got out of the car; she heard their footsteps. Then she was pulled out too. She was surprised that the touch had not been violent, as if she was being handled with utmost care; she came to know the reason soon enough. She wondered if this was a gang of kidnappers or local goons or just some unemployed first timers trying to earn a quick buck. She could think of giving them money and ask for release. After all, she was travelling with almost all her jewellery as suggested by her intelligent mother. She just wanted to be free.

The four sets of feet scampered back and there seemed to be someone else with them too. They addressed someone, a woman perhaps, 'Bai ji, piece *chek karleyo*. Look at the girl properly and check her figure. Don't complain later that we didn't give you a full piece. We'll charge you extra for her; she is *maal*.' She suddenly remembered her mother calling her Totta, the sexy object. Now she was actually being sold like a commodity. There was silence and she heard someone walking all around her. Then the same voice spoke, 'Touch her and see! She is a novelty. We'll not settle for less than fifty thousand. She will earn in lakhs for your returns and profit.' They all broke into shameless laughter while Rihana dreaded what was to happen next.

Someone took out the piece of cloth from Rihana's mouth and she fell down on her knees, pleading, 'Please leave me and my husband. We'll give you all the money that you want.'

'Shut up! How can we let go of such a prized catch? Your husband will rot in this garage forever; and if you don't comply with us or make too much noise, we'll kill him,' shouted another man. She heard a man being kicked and Veer crying out of pain. Rihana pleaded yet again, 'Please stop! Don't hurt him, please... Let us go. Whatever you want...whatever...I will make sure you have it... My family will give you all the money that you want.'

One of the four men said, '*Bade ghar ke lagte hain.* If we let them speak to their families, they will summon the police and we will be in trouble.'

A hand held her arm and pushed her forward; Veer also said, 'Where are you taking me? Rihana? Are you there?'

She sensed panic in Veer's voice and called out to him that she was with him and that he shouldn't worry. Wasn't this supposed to be his dialogue, she thought, but left it for later.

Someone pulled the blindfold off Rihana's eyes softly. When her eyes adjusted to the dimly lit room, she found herself in a dungeon. Veer was lying motionless in one corner with his back up against the wall. She looked at all the men around her, all three in front of her. They were dressed in black *pathani* suits and scarves covered their faces. They looked like goons straight out of underworld, the kind she had seen in the movies.

In the meantime, the man who had removed the blindfold came in front of her, gazed at her and then finally came up with a 'Eureka!' expression on his face. He said, 'Fine! We'll let you go; provided you give us all the cash and jewellery you are wearing. Rihana agreed immediately. She requested the man to untie her hands so she could remove her jewellery. She hurriedly took off her diamond earrings and pendant, the wrist watch that her parents had gifted her, anklets and the gold bangles she was wearing over the ivory ones. He came closer and said, 'Is that all? This will not be enough. We can't let you go.' Veer was witnessing all this in stony silence and after the man's comment said immediately, 'We have more jewellery in the car. We will give you all of that.' Rihana skipped a beat but at that time nothing was more important than her husband's life and her safety.

She told him he could take more if he promised to let them go. They all laughed and the man who seemed like their head asked her to come with him to the car and get the stuff. She emptied it in front of them and gave them every single piece of jewellery it had contained. All her diamonds, rubies, emeralds and pieces of gold jewellery changed hands.

He looked happy and contended. He went to the side and kicked Veer hard. Veer again cried out loud but slowly picked himself up. Rihana was relieved to see some life in him. Another man untied his hands and threw the car keys back at him. And they let them go. Just like that. The jewellery was worth a fortune, but these stones were just a commodity that had no significance for Rihana at that time.

Veer drove as fast as he could and Rihana didn't seem to mind the speed now. Once they reached the main road, Rihana asked Veer, 'Are you alright?'

Veer did not answer. He just focused on getting home.

'I think we should inform the police and also our parents,' suggested a petrified Rihana.

'Are you crazy? Veer screamed at her. They have let us go alive, that is more than enough,' advised Veer. 'This is not Jaipur, Rihana; this is Gurgaon and there are more goons than you can count.'

Veer's reaction perplexed Rihana, but she was in a state of shock to think or respond.

⚲

Veer unlocked the door and help it open for Rihana, 'This is our home now.'

Out of surging emotions and sheer relief, Rihana started crying. Veer pacified her and promised to make up for all the jewellery that had been looted. Jewellery was the last of her concerns as the horror of the episode was still fresh in her memory. Veer ensured that she ate properly and snuggled her into bed right next to him. Rihana was somewhat relieved at his gestures. She thanked all those gods again for the scary incident had only brought Veer closer to her in a good way. She hugged him and went off to sleep.

The next morning, both of them were up together. Rihana strolled into the kitchen to see the refrigerator full of fresh fruits and vegetables and all other essentials, all utensils of need neatly stacked. She fixed a quick breakfast for Veer and helped him get ready for work. He told Rihana before leaving that she should be ready in the evening; there was to be a welcome party for them in the Golf Club.

Veer seemed quite chirpy but Rihana was still upset with the happenings of the last evening and wanted to tell her parents about it. But she withheld that thought as Veer had asked her not to speak to anyone.

After breakfast, she took a short nap and then busied herself unpacking and setting her clothes and other essentials in the almirahs.

By the time Veer returned from office in the evening, Rihana was dressed in a pretty pink sari. After the horrible incident, that was the only time that she missed her jewellery. She wanted to wear some for the welcome party but had none. But she negotiated with that thought by thanking God for her and Veer being alive. Veer hurriedly took a shower and slipped into a fresh pair of formals. She was expecting a compliment but none came; so both of them got into the car and drove off to the club.

Just at the entry gate, their car was stopped by some men who Veer introduced to Rihana as his consultants. They requested both of them to step out of the car and walked them to a cycle rickshaw that was decorated with colourful balloons. Rihana was asked to sit at the back and Veer was made to cycle her to the main entrance. Rihana was amused to see Veer cycling a rickshaw in formals. Some dhol players walked along the rickshaw, with a few people dancing to its tune.

At the main entrance, Veer was asked to carry Rihana in his arms to where all his relatives and friends waited to welcome them. Veer did as he was asked to and Rihana was squealing with glee. Amidst much good-natured ribbing, they didn't allow Veer to put Rihana down. To top it all, he was even asked to do twenty sit-ups before he put her down. Veer tried his best, but doing that with a fifty kilogram woman in your arms is quite a task. Rihana's sari itself must have been a couple of kilos.

After much teasing, Veer was finally allowed to put Rihana down on her feet and he heaved a sigh of relief. He introduced her to all his relatives and friends. She was careful to wish all of them warmly, one by one.

Just as one of the men at the party crossed her, she almost choked. She was panic-stricken and gesticulated wildly to Veer until he was by her side. She whispered in his ear, 'Veer, I think he is one of those four men who robbed us....'

Veer looked at the man, then at her in surprise and said, 'No way Rihana, he is the HR manager of my company. His name is Prashant and he is very well off. What's wrong?'

Rihana had been deeply affected by the incident so she just thought of relaxing a bit.

Rihana felt very special with all the attention Veer's friends and relatives showered on her. She remembered to not indulge in too much conversation with unknown men, knowing Veer's temper well. Just when someone announced that the dinner was served, Prashant took over and announced, 'Ladies and gentlemen! To welcome Rihana into our family, we have a little surprise for her.' There was silence and Rihana was trying not to get perturbed by this man's presence.

Prashant continued, 'I request you all to adjust your seats to face the screen.' There was a sudden shuffling of chairs and every head in the hall stared in the same direction. The words echoed with finality, 'Rihana, this one is for you!'

The lights were dimmed and the screen came to life. Rihana saw herself and Veer being kidnapped, taken to the dungeon and everything else that had followed. She was suspended in disbelief for a few seconds before comprehension set in and Rihana felt like a complete fool.

'Oh my God! Oh My God!' she screamed and everyone else laughed. She covered her face with her hands, completely embarrassed.

Veer then walked to her with a box which she guessed would have all her jewellery and handed it over to her. 'I told you, I'll make up for it,' he said winking at Rihana.

The four dacoits were all his colleagues, including Prashant. They were the script writers, directors, producers, cameramen and actors of the movie, of which Rihana was the lead star.

'Thank you, Prashant! I'm sure your movie will be nominated for the Oscars. It's got all the right ingredients to win,' said Rihana, shaking hands with him.

'Rihana, we have built a bond with you. You'll remember this incident throughout your life...and lest you give us all the credit, let me tell you that your husband was hand-in-gloves with us, all through this abduction. In fact, he should get the Oscar for the best actor, for shrieking and getting kicked just the right way,' said Prashant and everybody around laughed.

He then handed over the CD of the movie to Rihana and said, 'This is a token of love for the new bride from all the bachelors in this room.'

Everybody clapped and for the first time, as Rihana leaned on Veer holding his arm, she felt a sense of belonging to him. Everybody in the gathering had made her feel so welcome and special. Rihana thanked Prashant and the other three boys and held the CD out saying jokingly, 'Hope you change your bachelor status soon, so that I can return this favour.'

§

Life fell in the usual humdrum with the passage of time. Rihana, like any other newly-wed, commenced with the duties she was expected to perform. She was cooking, keeping the house clean and running it smoothly, and most importantly, was looking after her husband. She, in fact, did everything that was expected from her as the lady of the house. Her mother was happy that she was settling in and was forgetting her fears slowly, and proud that she was proving her decision right.

The setting up of the new house, meeting new people, building new relationships, and attending social evenings and parties excited her. She was a good daughter-in-law too as she was in constant touch with Veer's parents and would often solicit recipes of Veer's favourite dishes and surprise him by bettering his mother's dish most times. So occupied was she with those new challenges that she found no time to take note of Veer's habits.

Desires and Denial

One day, as she sat near the window watching raindrops wash dust off leaves, she craved Veer's company. She wanted to start life afresh, with Veer. Now that the excitement of her new life had abated to a great extent, Rihana realized that she and Veer spent very little time together. Their interactions were restricted only to parties and food. Though she felt the gap widening with time, Veer showed no interest in her. Ever since they had arrived in Delhi, they had hardly had any intimate moments. Initially, Rihana did not worry too much thinking that Veer was probably tired or occupied with his official errands. She also remembered the gynaecologist's advice to abstain from sex for a few days. But it had been a while now and she had dropped him a few hints here and there. Her fleshly needs were growing and a woman's needs are no different from a man's. She was getting worried about Veer's disregard towards her needs, and more so, towards his own. Was he angry that his mother had chided him after their first time at it, she wondered. But then she also thought how a young man of twenty-six was not sexually attracted to a beautiful young woman of twenty-two, especially when she was his wife and wanted it equally.

In their infrequent bedroom romps, she had explained to Veer that she needed to reach an orgasm. But he was not patient to extend his moments of pleasure to please her.

For Rihana, an orgasm was an orgasm; there was no better word for it. She could relate everything else to an orgasm. But an orgasm could not be substituted with anything else. The kind of glow that an orgasm brought to her face, no make-up kit in the world could. She could have continued to watch porn and be content with her fingers, but then, what was the point of having a partner? It was like placing food in front of a hungry person and not letting him eat.

On one of the occasions of their togetherness, Veer just pushed Rihana aside after having enjoyed his moment of sexual bliss, saying, 'A woman does not need an orgasm every time, even *Kamasutra* says so. Then why do you clamour for it? I do not carry the patience to douse you with one each time we are in bed. Your craze for an orgasm drives me away from you.'

Rihana was stunned by Veer's blatant disclosure. The truth was now naked, and it was obscene and prejudiced.

'Where do I go for satisfaction then, Veer? It's my right to be equally pleasured when we are together. After all, I'm married to you and ensuring fulfilment of my needs is as much your responsibility as is mine. I've got my own expectations from this marriage. I just don't want to be carried around by you like a trophy-wife. I am frustrated most times because you leave me incomplete. All that I'm asking from you is good sex where I'm equally, if not more, satisfied. What's so wrong about that? And don't talk about my expectation driving you away from me; you have come close to me only when you felt the need for it,' Rihana had decided to confront it rather than simmer in anger for too long.

The gap between them kept growing with every argument they had; and they had an argument every single time Rihana was left unsatisfied. She felt suffocated in the void that was fast consuming both of them. It was only on occasions that Veer bestowed a sort of kindness on Rihana and let her be pleased, and that too when he was willing. Like the deserts imploring for rain, Rihana waited for Veer to get desperate for sex and consider her needs in bed.

On one such day, Rihana was sitting completely discontented, wondering where she had been going wrong with Veer. The peppy ringtone of her phone broke her reverie, and vainly thinking it could be Veer, she approached the phone slowly. But it was her Bua. She was in no mood to talk to anyone, but picked up with the hope that her mood would get better.

'How are you Rihana, my darling? It's been a long time since I've spoken to you. How is Veer? Hope he's taking care of you...'

Rihana had been hiding her pain from her mother all along; she did not want anyone worried, and what would she say. But hearing her Bua talk so lovingly, she broke down and began crying. There is nothing that hurts more than words, but then, there is also nothing that heals better than words; actions and implementation of those words follow much later.

'I'm alright, but I miss home. I miss you all, Bua,' snivelled Rihana. Her Bua consoled her and assured her she would settle down pretty soon and won't miss the family so much after a while. That Rihana had nothing to worry about. Though Rihana did not discuss anything about her married life, the wise old lady could see through her playacting. She was more experienced than Rihana and definitely more worldly wise. When a newly-wed couple has the woman frustrated, it could mean just two things – either it was beyond her expectations or too short of it. A concerned Bua had to find out.

So she did what she thought could have been the best damage control measure: she spoke to Rihana's mother. The latter first ignored the issue terming it as initial adjustment problems in a marriage. But later, as a concerned mother, decided to speak to Rihana about it.

'Rihana, I think you should pick up a job. You sit idle throughout the day and that is what makes you miserable. Get busy. Men run away even more if you pick fights with them. A job will keep you from fighting and help bring you closer to each other. Go out and get some fresh air every day.'

Rihana had not mentioned her marital frustration at all for she was shy in discussing it out with her mother. But she took her mother's advice seriously and spoke to Veer the same night. He had always been of the opinion that Rihana need not work for he was earning enough for their needs and luxury. But when Rihana told him that it could help take her mind off the problem at hand, and that it could help strengthen their bond, he relented for it to be a trial. He had not encouraged Rihana for it; he had *permitted* her to go out in search of work and join for just a trial period if at all she managed to find a suitable job.

She excitedly started looking for job avenues from the very next day. She had a Master's degree and would have loved to do something meaningful with it; plus, she had been handling her father's accounts for a long time. Veer had offered that she joins his work, but she had politely declined fearing that it could have turned the events the other way as well. A classified advertisement caught her eye. It was by a coaching institute and they wanted someone to teach young girls basics of fashion trends and designing. She also realized that working with girls at a coaching centre would not make Veer insecure.

She was called for the interview and the old lady interviewing her was sceptical about Rihana's non-experience. Rihana gathered herself up and used the tall lamp kept in the principal's room along with her dupatta and other accessories she could remove without compromising on her attire to create a fabulously designed dress. The erstwhile lamp now seemed like a mannequin dressed in a funky dress, complete with sunglasses and a scarf. Needless to say, she was selected and was asked to join immediately. She experienced happiness after a long time. Moreover, her long lost dream of playing with fabrics and colours was now coming true.

She cooked her favourite food that night and also kheer to celebrate the good news. Veer appreciated this decision and wished her luck. Rihana's mother had been right. Veer seemed to have been in need of a break from the daily frustrations brandished by Rihana. He was relieved that Rihana had something to do and hoped the job would keep her busy enough to not have too many expectations from him in bed at the end of a long, tiring day.

Now Rihana looked forward to mornings, to be able to go and interact with those girls. She had to do a lot of reading, especially the theory on design, since she hadn't had formal education in it. No doubt the job kept Rihana busy. It kept the fights low, but not her frustration levels; that kept rising nonetheless. The intimate moments went down, the need went up. The frequency of the fights reduced, but the intensity grew. The fights now had the ingredient of violent abuse, and they turned ugly. Older people say the couple that doesn't fight cannot stay in love. Fights do help in the process of conditioning and knowing each other better, but words spoken in rage render far more damage than can be undone and take you to a point of no return. Bitterness caused by Veer's ignorance of her needs had entered Rihana's veins as venom.

♦

Her students at the institute were young, vibrant and they all adored their new teacher. Plus, her colleagues were very supportive of her as a newbie and helped her in all possible ways. These things did compensate for her dissatisfaction with life, but not completely. Added to that was a bunch of chatty women in the staff room. She realized how obsessed some women were about men; they only spoke about their husbands. My husband this and my husband that.

'On my birthday, my husband gifted me Swarovski crystals,' said Rihana's colleague, Shipra.

'Oh, how beautiful!' was Babita's prompt and well-calculated reaction as her hands went to her mouth in fake awe.

Her fingers flaunted a rock and Shipra was tempted to ask her, 'When did you buy this ring, Babita? I love the design.'

'Oh, this one? This is my eighth anniversary gift from my husband,' replied Babita smugly.

Rihana had nothing to speak about her husband. She had plenty of precious metals and stones but they were mere objects for her. She would barter them for a content relationship with her husband, be it emotional, physical, or social, in that order.

She wondered if a diamond could give a woman as much satisfaction as an orgasm. She would rather have her husband be sensitive enough to want her to enjoy their sexual lives over diamonds any day.

Even with a job in hand, Rihana made sure to supervise the household work as usual. Her mother had asked her not to leave the work entirely to the household help. She would return home before Veer was back from office and cook.

'The way to a man's heart is through his stomach,' was a cliche she had often heard from her Dadi. So she cooked his favourite dishes and desserts, which sometimes earned her hearty compliments. She also garnered the support of Victoria's Secrets and the most enticing lingerie to seduce Veer. It reached the desired effect but the sessions didn't last beyond a couple of minutes, leaving Rihana embittered all over again. Nothing seemed to work on Veer. He had his priorities clear and didn't budge an inch to please Rihana. 'Giving' was not a word in his vocabulary. His habit of reaching a climax and then lying beside Rihana to snore while she wept in greater frustration was deeply annoying for her.

Three, and Counting...

Rihana had carefully chosen a baggy overall a couple of sizes too large for herself. She had been planning and looking forward to this day for some time now. As she stepped up on a portable ladder and picked up the brush dripping a vibrant pink into the bucket hanging on the side of the ladder, she flashed a broad smile. She had heard many men, and even women, compliment her on her enigmatic, colourful smile. She was going to use the same colour of happiness for redecorating the walls of her house today. With time, life had sapped all colour out of her life, and she was set to re-do it, in her way now.

She squeezed the extra paint off the brush on the sides of the bucket and looked up to see where to begin. She had to start from higher up to avoid any paint from trickling down unnecessarily. She was still formulating her thoughts, oblivious to the tall, broad, well-built man who had sneaked up behind her. He lifted her off the ladder with ease, and she shrieked as the brush kissed the floor instead of the wall. Though taken by surprise at first, she soon burst into giggles. His arms tight around her waist, and her feet dangling mid-air...that's how he carried her to the bedroom. The urgency with which he put her down and turned her to face him, she knew he wanted her. He held her close, in a grip that almost crushed her into him. It was in a split second that his mouth sought hers. Though flummoxed by the suddenness, Rihana welcomed him.

Veer had locked his fingers in Rihana's as his tongue locked into hers too, each exploring the confines of the other's mouth eagerly. When he forced her arms behind her fiercely, she was in pain. But the pain only accentuated her craving. Veer pulled her to him again, his hands locked into hers behind her back, aiding his movement. The incessant kissing, and their worked-up tongues flirting with each other was all it took for Rihana to be flooded with passion. She was moving to Veer's rhythm, as if performing a tango with the music of their hearts beating loud. She could feel him against her belly now, hard in his trousers. He let go of her hands and lifted her up to spread her on the bed. In his eagerness, he tore off a few buttons and hurriedly stripped the overall off to feast his eyes on her. This wasn't the Veer Rihana knew. It was also the first time ever that she saw him look at her with admiration.

Veer was mesmerized by her. He shifted his gaze from the delicious curves of her waist to the beautifully scooped navel from where a thin stream of brown hair emerged to spread into a velvety carpet between her ivory white thighs. A charm pendant in her waistband played mischievously on the brown carpet, occasionally kissing her valley seductively. Her shapely calves were provocatively alluring; her angelic feet just divine.

Veer had taken in each bit of her hungrily. And now, as adrenaline pumped faster in his blood, he nose-dived into her valley and started caressing her nub with his tongue. Rihana was now moaning in sheer ecstasy, and on cue dug her fingers into his hair, gently prodding him deeper. It was a little difficult for Rihana to accept such a drastic change. But her eyes reflected a craving: a desire of the mind that had gradually changed into a desire of the body. Her body was starved, and so was her soul. She knew too well that beggars could not be choosers, so she exulted in whatever came her way.

Veer looked up at her; her hunger was reflected in his eyes as well. Rihana unbuttoned his trousers and Veer quickly undressed himself and lay on top of her. He made her lie on her stomach and slithered upward from her back. He knew too well how sensitive her nape was and how it could take her to the edge in no time. He soon heard the moans go wild and felt her want reaching a crescendo. He rolled her to face him and ate at her ample breasts, the most bewitching part of her body. Despite being buxom, they were firm and seductive. Her nipples were blooming and supple and when he fervently kissed and savoured their nectar, she was aroused to further heights of ecstasy. She was now dripping and Veer could feel her juices and the thirst for a gala celebration. He reached down to her warmth and rubbed her sensitive spot, making her moan louder. To keep the loud moans in check, he sealed her mouth with his. He continued to play his magical fingers on her nipples and she herself took charge of her reservoir of happiness, her clit. She stroked it as Veer took care of her mouth and ample breasts till she shuddered into an orgasm. That was the third time in three months that Veer had been generous enough to give her one.

She was still panting in the afterglow when Veer moved. She knew well what was to follow and did not object. He slowly spread her legs, and glided into her depth with ease for she was overflowing with her own juices. In a few passionate strokes, she was moving to Veer's rhythm and was transported into bliss with her man inside her. He came out as quickly as he had gone in and Rihana cursed his inability to hold for the umpteenth time.

As he lay next to her, peacefully dosing into a siesta, she lay wide awake, thinking of the past and her relationship with Veer. A lot had changed in Veer and she was very happy about that change.

She dosed off into a slumber without realising and woke up to her phone ringing merrily. Veer had shaken her to pick up the phone; it was her Bua. She picked up the phone and went out in the living room to take the call.

Rihana was all joy when she spoke to her Bua; she was a satisfied woman that day.

'I'm glad to hear the cheerful Rihana, beta. What makes my girl so happy? Any good news?' Bua teased her.

She was so excited that she forgot what she was saying and chirped, 'No Bua, I got my third orgasm.'

Bua didn't know what to say, so she changed the topic, talked of family and Veer and hung up. She couldn't understand whether to celebrate with Rihana or feel pity for her. Unable to decide, she called up Preeti.

'Bhabi, are you aware of Rihana's condition? Veer and Rihana have been married for three months now. I don't think they are physically comfortable with each other yet. Today, Rihana sounded cheerful and I asked her the reason. She innocently told me that it was her third orgasm. The girl is suffering, I am sure. Love-making is a strong foundation of a marriage, and if Veer and Rihana are not yet comfortable with it, then the whole edifice of a happy married life will collapse.'

Rihana's mother was bent on not letting the smoke from this fire attract her relatives' gossip, and so she defended Veer, 'Shashi we know Rihana is an overindulgent girl. Being the only child in the family, we've coddled her a lot.'

Bua, however, didn't like that statement and retorted, 'In that case, you should have found a boy for her who could pamper her.

Bhabi, a marriage doesn't require pampering all the time. I have a strong feeling that there is something wrong somewhere.'

'But Shashi, Rihana is a very beautiful girl. No man will do a hundred laps of the swimming pool to marry a girl and then not be interested in her. I'm sure Veer loves Rihana. It's Rihana who should grow up and stop picking at small things. You know it well: fights put men off sex. These are just a few initial adjustment problems which will settle down with time and once they have a child they will get used to each other,' comforted Rihana's mother.

'Getting used to each other and loving each other are two different things, Bhabi. If he is saying "No" to a beautiful girl like Rihana, I suspect a bitter end. Any married girl deserves her husband's attention. Three months is a very small time for them to develop bitterness for each other. For almost a year after marriage, Sanjay and I did not even know the world existed beyond us. We were so into each other. And Bhabi, marriage is not only about producing babies, even dogs do that. We are all humans with each having a special need and *this* need can only be taken care of by your spouse,' she insisted.

This worried Rihana's mother for sure, but she didn't know how to resolve such a delicate issue. She had never spoken to her daughter over such matters. It was an awkward situation for her also. She thought of suggesting that Veer and Rihana go seek a marriage counsellor. A third party intervention, especially when neutral to both the parties, can work wonders in these situations.

☿

Rihana had become very close to Shipra in the little time that they spent together at the institute. She found that their common interest

lay in fitness and both of them ended up joining the same gym. Veer didn't allow Rihana to wear a swimming costume and swim after marriage for reasons best known to him; Rihana didn't retaliate and found another way to keep herself healthy and fit. Rihana and Shipra worked out together, and that acted as a motivation to them as well. Both of them enjoyed their workouts immensely and it usually ended up with a good chat. They discussed books, people, relationships, their students and everything under the sun that two women can be interested in. They bitched about the senior ladies at the club and their insecurities from young, pretty ladies like the two of them. The diversity in the conversations kept Rihana glued to Shipra, and the comfort let her speak her mind.

On one such occasion, the topic of their discussion was *change*, and how important and inevitable it is.

Shipra said in a philosophical tone, 'The only thing that is ever permanent is change. Every individual needs change and sometimes even when we don't need the change, it comes our way and we can't avoid it. If there is no change, life becomes monotonous; and if the change is too often, life becomes a struggle. What would your preference be, Rihana?'

Rihana thought for a while and then responded, 'I'd prefer life full of struggle. I like change. Monotony is irksome.'

Shipra said smiling at Rihana, 'Be careful what you wish for girl. You never know when He hears it all. By the way, how is Veer and how're you guys getting along?'

When Rihana didn't say anything, Shipra was quick to sense the silence. Sometimes, silence is more eloquent than speech. Plus, she herself had been married for long enough to know what could bother a woman.

Happily ~~Married~~ Marred

Veer told Rihana over dinner that his father would be coming to stay with them for some time. He said his father wanted to take a break from his mother, though jocularly. Rihana was very excited to hear this. She was sure of great company for a few days to come. Rihana promptly took a leave from the institute and went to receive her father-in-law at the airport in the afternoon, because Veer had a few meetings scheduled. They reached home and Rihana served him some pakoras with tea. Like Veer, his father was also fond of eating; it must be genetic, she thought.

She cooked a sumptuous meal for him and they sat chit chatting as they waited for Veer. He arrived pretty late but they ate together and discussed mundane things. Rihana showed Veer's father to the guest room but he insisted on sleeping on the floor, saying that's what he had done all his life. He repeated that he was more comfortable on the floor till Rihana gave in and spread a mat for him.

The next morning, Rihana wrapped up the household work, packed up Veer's lunch, served hot breakfast to both the men and left for the institute thereafter. It was a usual day and when she reached home in the late afternoon, she was exhausted. Papa was watching TV, she saw, and asked him if he had taken his lunch. He smiled and didn't say anything. She thought he must have waited for her and rushed into the kitchen to fix them both something to eat. She called out for the cook but was surprised to see that there were chapattis in the box and had been made not long ago.

'Who did this, Papa?' she asked, knowing that the cook only cooked under her supervision after she returned.

'I did it for you, my child. I thought you must be tired after a long day's work, so offered some help. This was the best I could do,' said Rihana's father-in-law with love.

'You could've let the cook do that for you. Why did you bother?' But he held that disarming smile for her and she melted, 'Oh Papa! You're a sweetheart. Veer is so unlike you. He never thinks of me. He will eat his food and then devour mine too, not realizing that I'll be hungry. He is a glutton. I don't mind that, but he should keep some for me too,' whispered Rihana. It had come out of her spontaneously and she didn't realise when it had taken the form of a complaint.

Rihana's father-in-law laughingly said, 'So what beta, you make some more. Or better still, order from outside. There is no dearth of anything for you. Whatever is Veer's is yours.'

Rihana didn't carry the argument further, probably because she could not express her thoughts and concerns to convince Veer's father of their son's irresponsible nature. So she preferred to leave it at buying more food for herself, as he had suggested.

The next day during the lunch break, which was mostly a gossip hour, one of Rihana's colleagues Meenakshi quipped, 'We heard your father-in-law is in town. So, how is it going? It must be really painful to have two men in the house.'

Rihana said, 'Not at all! I love his company; he is a gentleman. He even cooks for me, unlike his son. In the evenings, he recites verses from the *Ramayana* to me. I sometimes even dose off while listening because I am tired at the end of the day, but he waits the entire day for me to get back so that he can torture me with *Ramayana*.' She laughed indulgently, just like a child does while talking about a doting parent. She suddenly remembered something and quickly added, 'He even bribes me by cooking chapattis for me. *Namak khake gaddari?* Never. And what do old people live for? They just need someone to listen to them. At least I've got some company.'

And then digressing, she continued, 'What are you wearing for tonight's party Rihana? The theme is dare to bare or the ugly duckling.'

Rihana had not thought about the dress, but she was teeming with ideas. She was very innovative and good at creativity which was reflected in her setting up of the house and the lawn in the Delhi house. She could get the best out of even waste.

Once, while driving around Delhi for shopping, she had seen a man working with stacks of hay and jute. She invited that man to make her a small thatched hut in her lawn, which he agreed to do for a bottle of Old Monk Rum. She set up a small bar in that hut and for the bar stools, she got a labourer to give her three trunks of a tree. One third of each trunk was left buried in the ground and the rest was varnished to serve as a bar stool. A lantern was hung from the ceiling of the hut to give it a completely rustic look. There were many such pieces of art inside and outside her house.

For the party that night, Rihana dressed up as Ugly Betty of the well-known television series fame. She wore a purple sweat shirt with a pair of yellow track pants which were a complete mismatch. She wore her Nike shoes and used chewing gum and foil paper to make fake braces for her teeth. She wore old-fashioned, thick-rimmed glasses that brought about the desired effect. Since she had never dressed like that, many people in the Club just walked past her without recognizing her at all. On the contrary, Meenakshi was dressed scantily. The theme gave everybody a reason to break taboos. Most other parties saw these women in elegant saris and jewellery; but this one was bringing the other side of them out.

Looking at Rihana, Meenakshi said, 'What is wrong with you? I've never seen you like this. You've broken your glamorous image.'

'I never built an image to be broken; only you created it for me. How can I break something that you've created Meenakshi? But you look just splendid in this attire,' complimented Rihana.

Shipra looked at Rihana and showed her thumbs up. She appreciated Rihana's walk-the-talk of welcoming and creating "change". The party was held to celebrate one of the club members' anniversary.'

Whatever may be the occasion, drunkards always find a reason to drink. And that exactly was Veer's reason to drink. On many earlier occasions, Rihana had forbidden Veer from drinking as he could not carry his drinks. For Rihana, not drinking was better than making a fool of oneself, especially when it is a threat to one's wife. People at parties would wait for Veer to get drunk so that they could hit on Rihana. Rihana was needy, but not vulnerable.

Veer was sloshed, but this time, he took it to another level. He started making obscene gestures if the waiters were not quick enough to fetch his drinks. He flirted with any woman he came across. Some flirted back, while others had their sensibilities offended. And there were some who just looked at Rihana with pity in their eyes. That reaction made Rihana's pretty head explode with shame, embarrassment and anger, all at once. Luckily for

Rihana, most women were accompanied by their husbands who saw to ~~see~~ it that Veer did not cross too many lines of decorum.

After much drinking and to everyone's relief, Veer passed out. After the party, Prashant carried Veer to the car and put him next to the driver's seat. Handing over the car keys to Rihana, he said, 'I'm sorry Rihana, but Veer is not in a shape to drive. If you want, I'll drop you home.'

Rihana declined the offer saying, 'How will *you* go home then? It's already so late.'

There was nothing much for Prashant to hide. His colleagues and acquaintances knew Veer even before Rihana came into his life. They were aware of his habits and character, both. Rihana finally requested Meenakshi and her husband to drive ahead of her while she followed them.

She knew how to drive but wasn't a pro on Delhi roads.

Meenakshi and her husband were driving slowly enough for Rihana to stay close. When Rihana's house was just a couple of kilometres away, Meenakshi called her up and told her that they were to go into different directions from a point few metres ahead. Rihana couldn't ask them to drop her till home, so she thanked them and promised to inform her when she reached home.

It was a little past midnight and Rihana was sitting with a drunken husband who lay unconscious in the car. The entire area was isolated, shops were closed and dogs howled. The scene was spooky and Rihana developed cold feet. She was thinking about Veer and his behaviour that evening when a car zoomed past hers. She screeched to a halt, fighting her tears of embarrassment at Veer's behaviour. Right then, she saw four men approaching her car. This time, Rihana was sure that they were not Veer's colleagues. While one of them stood right in front of the car to stop Rihana from running him over, the other three tried to break open the windows and pulled at the door handles. The car was centrally locked and the doors didn't budge. Veer was still lying like a corpse. But just when they were going to deflate the tyres of the car, Rihana gathered herself and started driving. The man in front jumped out of the way as Rihana drove away. She honked at the entry gate of their housing complex while her heart pounded uncontrollably. The guards, heavy with sleep, opened the gates as fast as they could to the blare of her horns. They were finally safe inside the premises.

Rihana parked the car in front of her house and typed a one-word message to Meenakshi – Reached. Veer's father must have been waiting for them and came out. He saw Veer and helped Rihana to carry Veer out of the car, all the way to his bed. Veer puked on the bed the moment he was set on it. So at that hour, Rihana removed the bed sheet and cleaned it all up. Veer's father saw her do all this and looked defeated.

Once Veer was sound asleep, Rihana's father-in-law sat with her in complete silence. If he was in denial of Veer's excesses and his son's rocky marriage, the cloud was lifted now. He faced Rihana and said in an apologizing tone, 'I'm sorry, beta. I apologize on Veer's behalf. God knows that Veer's mother and I have brought him up with our values, sincerely. But he has somehow turned out to be a black sheep.'

Rihana could not hold her tears back now, 'I don't know how long I can do this, Papa. So many times, I have thought of coming to visit you and mummy when I could no longer stand his behaviour. But I know it's not right to burden you both at your age. And I cannot even go back to my own home. My parents will get very upset; my Dadi will be heartbroken.'

Rihana slept in the living room that night, and was off to work even before Veer had woken up.

She knew her colleagues would question her, and that was a bit to be handled smartly, she thought. Lost in all these thoughts, she could not prepare her father-in-law's breakfast as she was running late, and asked the cook to do so. She was the brave sort and knew she had to face some sniggers, but more than that the concerned eyes of her colleagues. She braced herself for the day ahead but soon realized that her fears were unfounded. None of her colleagues so much as lifted a brow or made any mention of her husband or the previous night.

Nevertheless, thankful for the sensitivity that her colleagues had showed − unlike her husband who could not think beyond drinks and women − Rihana returned home late in the afternoon. She saw Veer and his father having a discussion. Veer's father was advising him to be more responsible. Looking at Rihana walk in, Veer apologized to her with a guilty face. Rihana didn't need anything more. She was angry, but happy that he realised where he'd been wrong. So with the hope that he will do better the next time, the episode was buried.

That changed one thing though, Veer's father could not look Rihana in the eyes and talk. He was so ashamed of Veer and so fond of Rihana that he decided to go back to Jaipur. He accepted that the children were not happy together, but prayed for things to improve.

♀

Rihana spent a lot of time with herself as Veer was mostly travelling. He was planning to set up one more office in Kolkata which was an emerging market for real estate.

Rihana could not join him because of her job. Many a time she thought of quitting her job, but then retracted realising that her job was the only cause of her sanity and means of her survival.

Though as Veer's father had said, whatever was Veer's was hers too, but more frequently than not, Veer would carry all the ATM cards, including hers, with him and leave Rihana behind with no cash to run the house. She often had to take a part of her salary in cash or rush to the bank to withdraw what she needed for herself. She wasn't sure if Veer was doing that deliberately or if it was mere chance. But whatever the reasons were, it was quite tough for Rihana to do all the running around in the face of his ignorance and callous attitude.

One evening, Rihana was alone in the house, sitting in the living room, preparing some notes on designing theory for her class the next day. Veer was in Kolkata, not talking to Rihana enough over phone for her to know what exactly he was up to. Just then, the doorbell rang and Rihana wondered who it could be. It was Vikram Rai, Veer's colleague. When she opened the door, he had two envelopes in one hand and a huge empty bottle in the other. One of the envelopes contained Rihana's mobile phone bill and the other that of Veer's.

'Ma'am, these envelopes were lying in the office, so I thought of bringing them to you.'

After a pause, he continued, 'Umm, my water filter is not working. Can I have some water from yours?'

Rihana thanked him politely and took the bottle from his hand, asking him to come inside and wait till she filled the bottle.

'Where is Renu these days? Haven't seen her around,' Rihana enquired about his wife.

'She is at her parents' house for a few months. Our second baby is arriving.'

Rihana congratulated him while handing over the filled bottle to him. While taking the bottle from Rihana, he caressed her hand suggestively. She was uncomfortable with that gesture, especially when her husband was away. Just as women have very strong instincts; men can also smell a lonely woman from a fair distance. Vikram was just trying his luck, but his luck had no chance. Vikram got the clue and quietly took the bottle and left.

She closed the door and locked it from inside. While she was opening the envelopes to check the phone bills, the doorbell rang again. She went to the door to see Pankaj Mehra standing there with a book in his hand. Rihana smiled at him and invited him inside the house. He was pretty senior, so she was less threatened by him.

'I'd borrowed this book from Veer long back. I've finished reading, so thought of coming and returning it,' Pankaj said.

Rihana wondered why those thoughts never crossed their minds when Veer was around. She took the book from him and offered him tea, but he declined and said, 'Rihana, since Veer is away, you must come over and spend time with Ria and the kids. They will be happy to have you over.'

Rihana knew that the offer must have been conceived by Pankaj and Ria would have had nothing to do with it. These were the subtle glimmers from where the doors to adultery opened. Rihana had shut those doors with a lock on them and thrown the keys into the ocean. She did not want to exercise that option at all: first because she didn't want to hurt Veer's male ego; and second, she had learnt that lesson the hard way with Raj, that it was better to be chased without getting caught.

Once caught, the feelings of use, abuse and misuse start to sink in. Once caught, the woman loses the battle and she is tagged as 'available' forever. It was better to keep the men chasing than being caught. And men, they can never catch a woman without her consent and if they do, it is the most heinous crime, even in the eyes of God.

But what about a woman's needs? Just for these fears, should she continue to suppress her feelings and desires? A man could be on the prowl and hunt; if he gets lucky, he could even find his catch and feast on it. But a woman would be called 'fallen' if she ever tried doing that.

Rihana opened the envelopes and saw the bills. Her bill was just six hundred rupees. But she was shocked to find Veer's mobile phone bill – a whopping sixteen thousand rupees! Veer had complete powers over the finance of the house and this was a first timer for Rihana.

Back in Jaipur, her mother controlled everything in the house: from finance to her husband. She was bestowed with the absolute powers in the house and that absolute power never corrupted her. She always made sure that even a needle in the house didn't go waste. So seeing Veer misusing his power infuriated Rihana, but more than that, it shocked and surprised her.

When Veer came back to Delhi a couple of days later, Rihana gave him a warm welcome. She told him everything that had happened while he was away, including Vikram and Pankaj visiting their house. Veer was put on alert on hearing about his colleagues visiting the house in his absence.

'There is no need to entertain anyone when I'm not in the house,' thundered Veer.

Rihana had to raise her pitch to subdue him, saying, 'Then should I ask them to get out if they come knocking? You take me to all the parties and allow all the men to dance with me saying that "your wife's contribution" is a must in your business. You don't want to break any social ties and expect me to do so. You tell them all this, not me. It puts me in an awkward position. Veer, don't you realize that everybody is seeing through our unhappiness. Please try to change your ways. You are not a bachelor now, and I am your responsibility,' Rihana pleaded.

Veer, now fuming with anger, shrieked, 'What the hell do you want from me? I gave you whatever you wanted that night. Next time, no one should come to the house when I'm away.'

Rihana replied in a steely tone, 'Maybe if you were sober at all the social-dos, it would not send out the wrong message to men that I need taking care of, in bed and outside it. Do you realize that you should be angry with yourself instead of other men, because you are putting me in that vulnerable position. Besides, these are your best buddies trying to get me into their bed. Maybe you should talk to them directly instead of directing your anger at me!'

Veer swung his hand out to make contact with the right side of her face. And then the left. And then the right again. The blows on her face were excruciating; but the pain in her heart far worse. Veer walked out of the house and didn't return the whole night. Rihana was too shocked to worry where he was, and didn't care much at that time.

Veer came home in the morning, bathed and dressed in fresh clothes and left. She found a note on the bedside: "Flying to Kolkata". She was disgusted with this spineless man that she had ended up marrying. As a remedial measure for herself, she called in sick at work the next few days to nurse the bruises away. The showers she took were equally excruciating. She was unable to stop the copious tears that flowed under the hot water. She would sit down, unable to get up from the bathroom floor.

In spite of being in that deep daze of having experienced domestic violence, Rihana took some pictures of her face as the bruises turned from an angry red to an agitated purple and settled to a sad blue. She did not know what she would do with the pictures. She even contemplated sending these to her father, who would finally wake up from his slumber and help her. But who would help her if she would not. She decided to take it up with Veer when she saw him.

Six days after Rihana was assaulted by her own husband, Rihana decided to get her act together. She was slowly coming out of her shock and still had no real plan of action. She just knew that she had experienced a life changing moment, something that she thought only women in the slums or lower strata of society experienced – domestic violence.

When Veer was back, she didn't speak to him; nor did she confront him for the fear of being hit again. When Veer tried to speak to her, she evaded him, more out of anger than fear. One fine day, a few days after the incident, Rihana sent one of her pictures with the blue bruises to her father and father-in-law. She sent it separately to her mother with a message: "I tried and failed. I want to come home."

Both sets of parents discussed the matter – in hushed tones and raised voices – and finally decided to fly to Delhi.

Rihana opened the door and saw everyone standing there. She hugged her mother and a stream of tears flowed from her eyes. After she had cried for the longest time, she welcomed all of them inside the house and ordered the cook to bring some water followed by tea. In the meantime, Veer returned from his office and was shocked to see his parents and in-laws. He threw his bag on the side and excused himself after the customary greetings.

Veer's father was the first to talk when he joined them, 'Why did you do this, Veer? I demand an explanation.'

Veer put up a defensive act and looked at Rihana's mother while answering, 'Mummy, I have told Rihana N number of times to not entertain my colleagues when I'm away. But she doesn't seem to listen. Will you or my mother do the same if they were stopped by their respective husbands? When I tried to explain to her that men can have malicious intentions, she wasn't ready to listen and shouted back at me. Is it fair behaviour towards one's husband?'

Veer's questions raised a finger at Rihana's character in the presence of her own people. Hearing Veer talk like that infuriated Rihana. She had kept it all in for way too long now. She screamed out loud, 'Don't you dare cover up for this shit by this flimsy reason, Veer. Learn to be a man and face the truth!'

Veer refused to acknowledge her comment and instead pleaded to her parents, 'See, Mummy! That's how she behaves. She doesn't listen to anyone. I am glad you are here; maybe she will listen to you.'

Rihana had had enough! Her mother was going to say something, but she cut her words mid-sentence, 'Mummy! Just because he is my husband doesn't mean that I'm a slave to him. First, I haven't entertained anyone in a wrong way though he gives me enough reasons to do so; and second, I'll not put up with all this bullshit.'

Rihana's mother could not take it any longer; her daughter was putting her bringing up to naught in front of everyone. She walked up to her in anger and slapped her daughter right across the face. Rihana wasn't the sorts who would ask for any sympathy and behave like a victim. She was fighting for the right cause; maybe her approach had been wrong. She knew her mother was much concerned about her family image, but even she had not expected this from her.

Her mother said, 'If your husband doesn't want you to talk to someone, you shouldn't. There is no need to argue over it. Next time, I don't want to listen to any complaints of this sort.'

Just to balance out the whole situation, Veer's father got up and hugged Rihana and took her out into the other room. He spoke to her in a gentle tone, 'Beta, I understand that Veer is a tough boy but I'm sure you can win him over. When I was young, I too was very rigid but your mum-in-law took good care of me and I changed. People change. It's all in your hands. Women are stronger than men in all respects. Keep patience and I will warn Veer not to lift his hand on you again. If he does, I'll thrash him to pieces. But before that, you have to promise me to be patient with my boy.'

Rihana respected Veer's father more today than her own mother who had chosen her family image over her daughter. She didn't argue any further as Veer's father's words had acted like a balm on her wounds. She learnt the hardest lesson of her life that day, 'One never wins a battle through anger.' She had lost before she had even started. By evening, everything seemed settled and both the fathers decided to take the family out for dinner. The next evening, they all left for Jaipur.

§

Her students, her routine at the gym, and Shipra's company rejuvenated her quite a bit. While resting in the staff room on a busy day, Rihana was left upset when one of the senior teachers asked her to be dressed in a sleeved blouse and not a sleeveless one.

The same evening, she got talking to Shipra about this incident in the institute and asked complainingly, 'Why are we restricted from wearing what we want? When I was in school, my mother kept me covered because of the fear of men. When I moved here, Veer had a problem with me swimming in a swimming costume. I can hardly wear a burqa to the pool, so I decided to gym instead of swimming. Now all the senior ladies behave like our mummies and want us to be covered. I don't know when I will be able to wear what *I* want to, rather than what *others* want me to. Whether covered or bare, men will look at you anyway. Probably a woman should not bother about dressing for a man, because no matter what she wears to impress him, he is always mentally undressing her.'

Listening to Rihana complaining thus, Shipra also poured out, 'It's got nothing to do with the men here but the old fat hags who want to protect and possess their husbands. For them, marriage and producing children is the only mission. Till then, they will maintain themselves. The moment they deliver a baby, they accumulate to a grand total of some eighty-ninety kilos. What will the poor husband do, if not look around? So in a way, such women are catering to their husbands' fleshly needs only, not psychological. Those oldies get an erection looking at women like you and me and then trouble their asexual wives. These ladies asking you to not wear sleeveless is not because of any decorum crisis or other bull-crap like that; they just want to avoid the grief of their men troubling them for sex. A man helps a man, but a woman – she's the woman's biggest enemy.'

Rihana was flabbergasted to hear that and stared at her nails blankly.

'But why do you look so pale?' digressed Shipra.

Rihana thought for a moment if she should share it with her, but decided not to hide anything. In any case, her life seemed to be an open book now; after the party everyone knew what was and wasn't between her and Veer. She would merely be filling in the gaps for Shipra.

'I do not know where to start Shipra, it's a very, very long story,' said Rihana.

Shipra was waiting for her friend to confide in her. She did not know how to intervene as most marriages were strictly between the two families concerned. Nevertheless, she could already see the tell-tale signs of abuse, neglect, alcoholism, and deep cultural divide in her friend's marriage. Shipra patted her hand and quietly suggested lunch at their favourite restaurant.

When they met up at the restaurant, it was as if a dam of emotions had burst open. For the first time in her eight months of being married to Veer, Rihana was finally able to tell someone what she was feeling.

'I have been to hell and back ever since I got married. Besides, now you all know this too, Veer has the most erratic behaviour I have seen in a person. Sometimes, I feel he has a split personality; his behaviour is beyond my comprehension. He keeps a very tight tab on any money spent on the house, he will not let me spend a penny on myself, and yet, his phone bill is *sixteen thousand rupees*! I survive on my salary and the money my Dadi keeps sending me now and then in the name of some festival or celebration.

'He is so protective about me that I fail to understand what the hell is he protecting me from! No one can dare to touch me without my permission, you know. So it isn't that I am a *bechari ladki* who he has to save.'

Shipra was not shocked to hear this; Veer had made his behaviour quite public. Plus, some men tend to get over protective with their partners.

Rihana was teary-eyed now, 'I had different expectations from marriage, Shipra. I don't know if I should be telling you this but, I found him watching porn and pleasing himself in my absence. And yet, he hardly seems interested in me in bed. It's humiliating that he does this to me, if only to please his ego or whatever reason he can think of. I can almost count the number of times we have had sex since we got married, and even on those rare occasions, there's honestly nothing in it for me. He is the only one who is satisfied.'

Shipra was confused at this confession of her friend, 'That's strange. How can Veer say no to a girl like you? You are the manifestation of any male's fantasy and this compliment from a girl carries more weight than any man's opinion. What else can a man ask for, a horny wife?' Both of them giggled at their bawdy talk.

Shipra and Rihana finished lunch and started for home, not before Shipra gave her a hug and told her that what she was feeling was not overreaction. Rihana felt better after sharing it with her and knowing that she was not being overly emotional.

After the parents had gone back, Rihana did not, for the first time, try to make things work. She wanted to see what Veer would do. And as she had expected, he did nothing. Though he stayed home for a month before leaving for Kolkata for the final deal for his office there, things between them remained cold. Rihana was again lonely.

While Veer was away, Rihana's mother came from Jaipur to see her and give her company for a few days. Veer knew of this plan and didn't mind because he was more or less sure that Mummy would instil some sense into Rihana.

On the day of the flight, Rihana picked her up from the airport. They didn't speak all along the long journey from the airport to Rihana's house. When they finally reached home after Rihana successfully manoeuvred the vehicle through the crazy traffic, her mother was pleased to see her daughter's house set up so tastefully. She had not paid attention the last time because of various things on her mind. Even what little she had noticed, she had refrained from complimenting Rihana.

'You've decorated the house really well, Rihana,' this time she was generous.

'Mom, I dream of a home where people are happy. This, what you see, is a house that has a skilled decorator. The souls dwelling in it still remain ugly.' She left to get water and prepare for tea and snacks.

Rihana's mother held her hand and sat next to her, asking politely, 'Aren't you happy, my child? I just thought you are pampered and that's why Veer is having trouble adjusting with your ways.' Rihana saw genuine concern in her mother's eyes this time around, and since she had been slapped the last time, she knew smartly chosen words would do better than anger.

'Mom, I am just not able to understand Veer's predicament. You said men distance themselves when women fight; but I don't. Trust me! Then I wonder why is he irritated with me all the time. Have I done something wrong? Am I not pretty enough to get his attraction?' lamented Rihana.

'No, my child! I know you are doing your best. But marriages are like that only. You have a name and a societal status of being married. Why do you cry?' Rihana's mother said consoling her daughter while she cried her heart out.

Rihana hesitated for a moment but told her mother in detail what had happened the last time, which Veer had twisted for his own benefit and Rihana's anger had messed up. She watched as her mother's expression changed from shock to horror, followed by melodramatic tears. She hugged Rihana and cried bitterly for what her daughter had been through.

But, till the end of her almost week-long stay, Rihana's mother dished out exactly the same advice that she had given her daughter before the wedding: If Veer continued to make her unhappy, she would ask Papa to call for a meeting between the families to intervene on Veer's violent ways. However, it amused Rihana in a sad way that her mother had conveniently omitted the one line from that pre-marriage speech, that bit where Rihana could come back to her parents anytime if she was not happy with Veer.

It was crystal clear to Rihana that her societal status was just pruned to be within the confines of a marriage by her mother. She didn't look beyond; neither allowed Rihana to look beyond. It was considered more important than her feelings and longing for love and concern.

Love Games and Loveless Affairs

It was on the fifth day of Rihana's mother's stay in Delhi when they got the news: Veer's father had suffered a heart attack. Rihana's mother left for Jaipur immediately, though her father was there in case something was needed urgently. Veer had instructed Rihana to stay in Delhi and wait for him. But as reason would allow, it made no sense for Veer to come to Delhi first, so he flew directly to Jaipur.

Rihana had suggested the same to him; it would have been easier for her to fly back with her mother but he had had his way. What with her mother supporting his reasoning blindly! After his father's condition had stabilized, the doctors suggested that he be put on a pace maker as he had developed Arrhythmia. For better treatment, he was shifted to Fortis Hospital in Delhi.

Rihana had been very restless to see him; she had been extremely upset about his health and longed to see her father-in-law. She asked Veer many times if she could join him or come to see him, but he declined. What added to her misery was Veer's renting a room in a hotel close to the hospital rather than let his mother stay at their home.

While everyone in the family was struggling to come to terms with these erratic happenings, Veer's uncle passed away. There was utter chaos in the family as the deceased was Veer's father's younger brother. Veer being the only son in the family was supposed to perform all the Hindu rituals for his uncle's death in Jaipur. He instructed Rihana to stay home for he had to freshen up before leaving. He went to Jaipur to light the pyre of his only uncle and returned the same evening. There was to be the *bhog* on the fourteenth day, so Veer's mother returned to Jaipur.

Rihana could not hold back anymore, and although Veer had been asking her not to go to the hospital for some reason, she still went ahead and met her father-in-law. The old man was very happy to see her. When Veer came to know, he bit on his anger in the hospital but unleashed it at home. The whole anxiety of her father-in-law's health combined with Veer's behaviour led to a breakdown and she fell down unconscious. She had to be hospitalized for two days on account of this anxiety and Shipra was the only one looking after her.

When after a few days, Veer's father's condition stabilized, he returned to Jaipur. Not once did Veer offer that he comes to stay with them, but Rihana proposed accompanying them back home. Veer returned to Delhi a couple of days later, and Rihana remained with her in-laws for a couple of weeks to help her father-in-law recover. She also went to see her parents every now and then but didn't discuss anything about Veer with them. She knew they were too occupied with their image in society to wonder what their daughter had been going through. During those visits, she also discovered that her grandfather had not been keeping too well. He had grown weak and now needed assistance for his daily chores. Rihana shuttled between her grandfather's and in-laws' house to keep both the sides happy as both desired to be with her. In many ways, Rihana was a lucky girl. But where she had required her luck the most, in her marriage, she was the most unlucky.

When Rihana came back to Delhi, she found a different Veer waiting for her. He started interacting with her more, asked her about her work and students. He would take her out to restaurants and movies. Things that had fallen apart, he was now trying to bring them together. Rihana was more surprised than pleased. These outings were followed by great sex sessions; this was making her life complete. Everybody around her noticed a pleasant change in her; she was smiling more, dazzled everyone with her radiance and was more creative at work too.

'Rihana, you are glowing. Are you pregnant?' was a question she commonly faced these days, especially by the elder ladies in office who grew a bit more insecure.

People might have had their own definitions of a 'happy married life,' but for Rihana, it meant a contended body and soul. Good sex between two people was a result of good bonding, and it in turn strengthened that bond too. She cared a fig for diamonds, houses and cars; she just wanted to be happy with her mate. Was it too much to ask for?

Rihana was one of those rare girls who defied the notion that sex was a man's prerogative. She had to wait for love, but till then, she preferred sex. And why not! She could gather that although good sex may not lead to love, but the physical bonding and addiction to the other person is a big reason to make them stay in the relationship. Who says that if you can't have sweets, don't have salt too?

Rihana had been enjoying her special evenings with Veer so much, that she totally forgot all else. She had a busy schedule at the institute and couldn't really catch up with Shipra. So on the third day, when Rihana landed up at the gym, Shipra asked her surprised, 'Where have you been? No gym for three days!... And see what happened. You seem to have put on weight. What the hell is happening to you?' She sounded amused.

'In this age of slim fit and size zero, Sonakshi Sinha is my only hope,' Rihana giggled and got on to the treadmill to run her daily marathon.

After their workout, Rihana and Shipra walked home together and resumed their daily dose of talks. They had to cover up the backlog of three days.

Now, talking is also therapeutically orgasmic for women. But the tragedy is the same: they need someone to do it with.

Rihana was unstoppable 'Shipra, Veer has changed.' She confided with a lot of excitement in her voice and continued, 'Veer is taking me out to the movies and we have eaten out all the three days. Now he makes advances instead of me going to him. You know my score: it is fifteen now! I don't know what has brought this change, but I'm not complaining. I guess when you give up on things and don't think about them, they follow you.'

Shipra was happy to see Rihana beaming with joy. She genuinely felt happy for her and said, 'I'm glad to know that your insatiable lust is being adequately suckled.' Both of them hugged in the middle of the road and oozed happiness. Shipra was quick to add, 'But jokes apart, men in general have an authority over sex. They restrict uninhibited sex only to prostitutes and abandon it for aesthetic women, so that they never grow beyond it. Maslow wasn't a fool when he created the pyramid of needs. One can't completely enjoy the next level till the basic levels are achieved satisfactorily. Sex need is at the base of the pyramid, you know, along with the other basic needs like food, water and air. We women never grow beyond our sexual needs. Our groove is stuck at the sex need and therefore, we take time to match up with the men to reach self-esteem needs or any other need on the higher levels. It's a still bigger problem for those women who know and have experienced sexual bliss. A vast majority of women are ignorant about this too. It's a wrong notion that sex is a problem for men, it's a bigger problem for women because men never understand. Men biologically release with more ease.'

Rihana had heard her out patiently, 'I am not saying I have inadequate self-esteem on my personal and professional levels. All I am saying is that I can deliver better if my physical needs are taken care of.' Shipra nodded and Rihana added with a wink, 'I don't know if it's a man's problem or a woman's problem, but the solution for all problems is a fucking good orgasm.'

⚘

It was Veer's birthday and Rihana had planned a surprise for him. She had made all the preparations single-handedly and he didn't have a clue. She had even ganged up with Prashant to ensure that Veer came home before midnight and didn't stop in office for anything. She knew Veer had wanted an Armani leather jacket for a long time and it was the perfect occasion for Rihana to gift him one. So she sat on the bed waiting for Veer, with only the jacket on.

Veer opened the door a little before midnight, and saw Rihana... in the jacket alone. While sipping a glass of wine, she asked him, 'The naked girl or the jacket...what would you like to have for your birthday?'

Veer was excited about the jacket and Rihana, and both of them together just made the session steamier. They undressed each other, though he didn't have to do much. Rihana took off Veer's trousers and mouthed his manhood. Veer stopped her for the fear of coming early. He wanted to ensure that Rihana got feasted first. He licked her wetness till she was flooded with juices. When he put his finger inside her velvety tunnel and stroked it, Rihana started moaning. Veer was used to her moans by now, but still objected. And though Rihana didn't want the flow to break, she was conscious about Veer's apprehensions concerning the noise. She preferred to keep her moans under control; she didn't want to fight a battle that was going to end in her loss. The ensuing battle to reach an orgasm was far more lucrative. Veer was now at work on Rihana's nipples. He sucked and licked them gently while she toyed with her clit with her legs spread wide open. Only when she was about to come, she could not hold herself any longer and moaned Veer's name with extreme pleasure, 'Oh Veer... Happy birthday!!' She was thankful to Veer for being patient and to reciprocate, she turned around to get on her knees to let Veer enter her from the rear, making her bend on her all fours, just the way he liked. Veer slid his firmness into her, and within a few seconds, came out. By the time they finished, both were sweating and panting.

As Rihana and Veer lay beside each other, she folded her hands to thank God for that new lease of life with Veer. No sooner had that thought crossed her mind that Veer's mobile buzzed. Rihana knew his friends would want to wish him, but the way Veer jumped on the phone and cut the call in panic made Rihana curious. The silenced phone had ominously set her mind ringing.

'Who was it, Veer?' she asked politely. 'Someone dying to wish you?' She rolled onto her side to look at him.

'Prashant must have called for some work,' he stammered.

Rihana did not feel any better with that answer and decided to take things into her hands. She had already spoken to Prashant and knew that he would not have called.

She rolled to her back and picked up her mobile from the side table. 'Hi Prashant, I'm sorry to have called you this late in the night. Did you just call Veer? Is he required in the office?'

Veer had started sweating now, and Rihana was getting impatient. She turned to Veer and said, 'Prashant didn't call. Who called you Veer?'

'It must be didi from London. Some unknown number yaar. Why are you ruining such a beautiful moment?' he said getting up from the bed and rushing to the bathroom.

'The moment has already been ruined. And if didi was calling, I think you should call her up,' insisted Rihana.

'I don't have international calling service on my mobile,' Veer called out from the bathroom.

Rihana picked up her mobile and dialled her sister-in-law. She had to tell Veer that she was no fool and he should take her more seriously.

'Hello Priyanka didi! How are you?... How is everyone at home?.... That's nice... Yes, we are all fine... Oh, did you call up Veer by any chance?... Oh okay! No problem... Yes, we will. You all also take care.... the birthday boy is in the washroom... Yes, I will ask him to call you. Okay... bye.'

Veer could see trouble written all over her face when she said, 'Veer, it wasn't didi too. Who was it then? And please don't doubt my intelligence by telling another lie.' Veer was being defensive and only the guilty behave that way.

Rihana was suspecting malice because she knew very little about Veer; he never opened up and Rihana never dug. But she didn't want her suspicion to remain a mystery forever. She knew suspicion would haunt her forever and if Veer was guilty, it would haunt her all the more. How could a new life that Rihana was experiencing with Veer lately, nest on suspicion? She had to rule out suspicion, and for that, she had to find the truth. She was only scared of the fact that if she found the truth with Veer being guilty, then the reality that she had conceived so far would turn into an illusion.

She waited for the blow to fall.

'She is *just* a friend. Her name is Ishika,' muttered Veer.

The *just* had done the trick for her. Rihana had nothing except Veer's reaction as the foundation of that uneasy feeling inside her. But she trusted her instincts which foretold signs of betrayal.

Rihana quickly put on a night dress and went to the other room to sleep. But sleep was elusive; it danced like a mischievous memory that she wanted to confront. Where had she gone wrong? She looked good, she cooked well, she was also good in bed, and above all, she trusted Veer.

The next morning, Rihana called up her Mom and told her about the incident. 'Would you still think the same about me and Veer?' She didn't get an answer.

Rihana didn't know who to talk to. She hadn't spoken to Tamanna in a long time, although they were in the same city. Shipra would make her comfortable, while Tamanna would probably just go and kill Veer, but she needed advice from someone in the family. Dadi, she thought, would be too vulnerable to pain on her account. So she called up her Bua, who heard her out patiently.

'Rihana, it's your life and your life is a result of the decisions you take. I won't impose my decisions on you. If you want to confront Veer more than this, do that. If you want to stay with him, you stay; if you want to come back, it's up to you. Whatever the decision, I'll support you. But you have to be accountable for your decisions.'

And Rihana was ready to face the aftermath of her decision. She couldn't believe Veer being happy not because of her, but another woman.

When she gave Shipra her resignation letter, she advised, 'Rihana, you might change your mind later. Instead of resigning, you take leave for a month. Don't give in to your emotions. Instead, give yourself time to think this over and then take an appropriate decision.'

Rihana didn't argue and handed over both the resignation letter, and the leave application to Shipra. Within an hour, Shipra and Rihana were back home, packing her stuff. Shipra dropped her at the airport and wished her well, with a promise to stay in regular touch. While bidding goodbye to Shipra, Rihana remembered their conversation about "change". Rihana's wish had come true.

℮

Nobody came to pick her up at the airport this time. But thanks to Veer, she had given up on expecting being pampered now. She took a taxi to her house. She was treated with sympathy but was not welcome. Her parents were too worried about their image; they wanted her to stay with Veer.

Rihana's mother called up Veer and asked him to come to Jaipur immediately. He arrived after ten days, his parents and sister in tow. By that time, Rihana had all the details of Veer's phone bills. He was in thick soup now; the bill details were conclusive evidence against him revealing his relationship with Ishika. All these days, Rihana had not spoken a word of it to anyone. She decided to talk only after Veer and his family arrived.

∮

She confronted him in front of all others, her parents and his, 'Veer, I know the truth.'

There was silence. After a pause, she continued, 'I just want to know the truth from you.'

She behaved like an interrogating officer who had more than the life of a culprit in her hands.

Veer opened his bag of lies and said, 'I met the girl on Facebook.'

Rihana kept calm. 'I'm listening,' nodded Rihana.

Veer looked embarrassed to explain things in the company of his parents and sister but continued, 'Then, I asked for her number and spoke to her. She is a student in college in Delhi. I have been in touch with her since last October.'

'She is a student, Veer. Consider her age and yours!' Disgust was dripping from her voice, 'And your phone bills clearly show how long and how many times in a minute you have called her up. Did you have any serious relationship with her?' probed Rihana.

Veer continued with guilt that was not only writ large on his face but was even reflected in his tone. 'Sometimes we spoke salaciously, and...then...'

Rihana cringed at the thought. But she had found out something else too. She had to let the cat out of the bag, 'And why didn't you let me come and see Papa in the hospital? Tell us all why you didn't let Mummy stay in our home and rather put her in a hotel?'

Veer looked shocked at these questions. He sensed Rihana had dug deep and wanted this to end now. He was guilty, as charged.

He spoke apologetically, 'When daddy was in the hospital and mummy had come back to Jaipur for uncle's bhog ceremony, I called her to the hotel we had booked and she spent two days with me. I swear, whatever happened in those two days...I'm really sorry about that.'

Listening to her husband's shameless acceptance, Rihana broke down. She felt humiliated and hurt. When Veer got up to console her, she screamed, 'Don't touch me, you scoundrel. What wrong did I do to you that you made me suffer like this? I did everything for you: managed your house, cooked for you, did all that you wanted me to. And you did all this when your uncle was dead and your father was almost dying? You live for yourself only; you are selfish and a debauch.'

Rihana was perhaps just over reacting to something that men usually do, and do without remorse. Perhaps it was not as traumatic for the people listening, but for the two in it, nothing in the world could cure their suffering.

Both the families had been hearing it all: Veer's shamefacedly, Rihana's worriedly. Her family was concerned about Rihana's health as she had not eaten properly for many days and had grown very weak. On top of that, she was fighting the biggest battle of her life which wasn't chosen by her.

Rihana contained herself and faced Veer again, 'I want to meet that girl. And whatever you have admitted, I want it in writing, that too on a notarized stamp paper. If you don't fulfil any of the two, I'll have to speak to my lawyer.'

At this, Veer's sister Priyanka took offense and became the official spokesperson from his side of the 'Rihana, what is done is done. He is after all a man. Men will have these little escapades. We just ignore them and move on. Is it not enough that we have all come to pacify your ego? Why do you want Veer to bring that girl in? And none of my business, but it's usually when men are not getting love and affection at home, that they seek it from outside. So in some sense, you have contributed to his digressions.'

Rihana knew too well to not fall into this trap where society decides to question the woman on every fault of the man. Or get into a discussion about her contributions in forcing her man into an illicit affair! She was only glad that it was not Veer's parents who had spoken thus; she still felt deep respect for them.

She ignored her sister-in-law's tirade as she had done all that and more than what she thought took to make a marriage work: from pampering her husband with his favourite dishes, to keeping the families' name intact; from tolerating his ridiculous public behaviour, to his complete ignorance of her. Even if he would have asked her to sexually please him for an entire day without reciprocating in a similar fashion, she would have done that without asking for anything but concern in return. Veer was undoubtedly insensitive towards Rihana's needs. She repeated to Veer in an emotionless tone, 'Notarized stamp paper and the girl. *Now!* Or you will hear from my lawyer.'

Veer was caught between the devil and deep sea. He chose the lesser of the two evils and agreed to Rihana's demands.

The families dispersed and Rihana refused to speak to her parents; she knew not what reconciliatory ideas they might be garnering. Veer, in the meantime, spoke to Ishika and made arrangements to fly her to Jaipur for a day. They met at Rihana's house and she was shocked to see Ishika. She was so ugly that Rihana was reminded of someone on whom a spell of staying ugly had been cast. Even if not by looks, Ishika was indeed the ugliest woman for Rihana as she had turned Rihana's life into hell.

Rihana's mother saw the colour fade out of Rihana's face and spoke for the first time, 'Out of all the girls in the world, you found *this* girl to sleep with. Just look at my daughter and look at *her*. Veer, I stood up for you, even against my own daughter. You've let me down. I'm ashamed of myself and you.'

Rihana was baffled at what her mother had just said. She seemed more upset because of the choice of the girl than Veer's affair. How Punjabi mothers are obsessed with good looks!

Ishika might not have been the prettiest girl in the world, but she was young and had some self-respect. Being called ugly by two women, in front of the man she had trusted so much, gave her some tough time too. Tears flooded her eyes and she dug her gaze into the floor near her feet. Rihana questioned her, 'What made you sleep with my husband?'

She replied amidst sobs, 'I didn't know he was married. Believe me, please. In fact, he tricked to get me here also.'

That's when Rihana wondered as to why she was cursing that girl. If Veer could lie to her, he could have done that to the poor girl too. The enemy was her own husband. The girl had corrupted Rihana's marriage unawares; but Veer had known it all along. She walked up to the girl and told her, 'Now you know he is married. What do you have to say?'

She said earnestly, 'You are like an elder sister to me and I am sorry to have done this to you, even if unknowingly. I would have slapped this man here, but I wouldn't dirty myself with his touch now.'

Rihana could sense the shock the girl was going through and requested her to leave. Ishika told her she didn't have money to go back to Delhi because she was a student.

Rihana handed her some cash for the ticket and called out to Roop Chand to drop her where she wished.

Veer left soon after, with a faint apology and a whispered request for Rihana to come back with him.

She wondered what a fool that girl was to trust Veer in just a few months to agree to come with him. But then she looked at herself – she considered herself a bigger fool who had trusted him for a lifetime by marrying him even after knowing that he was not the man for her. She regretted the decision that she had taken for her mother and society at large. Only if she had not given in to her mother's tears, she would have never faced this misery.

When Ishika left, Rihana sat down on the couch, lost in thoughts. She looked up at her Bua who was feeling miserable for her niece. Rihana's pained eyes made her speak, 'Rihana, my sympathies are with you, beta, but that's how men are. When it comes to their balls, their brains stop working. I know it's hard for you to accept now, but let it go! Let it not bother you so much, my dear.'

Rihana knew what all men could do just for some fun in life, but she had her own reservations about whatever had happened. She said, 'I know that Bua, but he did all this at the cost of my happiness, *our* happiness. Why couldn't he give me the time I always wanted from him? First, he doesn't give me time, and second, he gives my share to someone else. I'm aware that these things happen, but he should have given me some love and attention. Then he also wouldn't have felt the need to do all this.'

To which Bua replied, 'For all you know, Rihana, he could have been an equal ass in bed, even with that girl. Men go to such women to boost their own ego. If I were in your place, I would be happy. You should relax now; he has given you all the reasons to be out of an unhappy relationship.' Rihana looked up at Bua, realising the impact such a decision could have. But Bua continued more assuringly this time, 'I would still prefer that you stay in it. But if that makes you too unhappy, the choice is yours. We can only support you in your decisions.'

Her mother tried to talk to her into going back to Veer. But she was firm. She was now convinced that the change in Veer was only due to the scum bag's guilty conscience.

♀

Veer's family and colleagues called Rihana to convince her to come back and sort out the issue. Prashant called her and said, 'I don't know what to say, Rihana, but I'm deeply hurt.'

Rihana said in a broken voice, 'Prashant, I only wish I was never introduced to Veer.

'I'm sure things will get back to normal. Sometimes, it's just time that plays tricks in a relationship. At a given time, one is expecting something and the other is expecting something else. When a wife wants to spend time with her husband, he is setting up his career; and when the husband wants it, the wife is either pregnant or busy with the kids. Their priorities never match. For one, the priority might be love and for the other, money. It requires constant work to keep a relationship going and it's very difficult. The timings of expectations fail to match and that is what causes all the problems. I didn't want any problems for myself, nor wanted to create any for the other person, I chose to stay single. I am not saying I am taking Veer's side; he has definitely made a mistake. I just pray that a time comes when you both are with each other,' said Prashant and wished her luck for her life ahead.

A lot of other people called up Rihana to ask if she was getting back with Veer. They also asked her the reason for her annoyance with Veer and why she had left suddenly. She was not interested in giving explanations of any kind. Some battles were not worth fighting, she knew. If she didn't give any reasons for leaving Veer, people would have bestowed titles such as high-headed, arrogant, immature and impulsive bitch on her. And if she gave reasons, then the question was, "What was lacking in you that he went out?" It was a *Catch-22* situation for Rihana and therefore she preferred keeping quiet and restrained herself from giving any explanations.

People were not even concerned; they were just thanking God for not putting them in a situation like Rihana's. It was a poison for Rihana to swallow and only she had to find an antidote to it.

Reclaiming the Lost Self

Rihana was a chirpy girl and a favourite with friends and relatives. She had maintained good relations with everyone, at least till she got married. So when she contacted a few friends and relatives, they were all ready to help her. Somehow a damsel in distress is a darling to both men and women, though for different reasons to each.

Now that Rihana had decided to take her time to decide about going back to Veer, out of all the options available to Rihana to move further in life, she chose her mother's suggestion. She agreed to move to Mumbai to her uncle Dr Vishesh Verma – a renowned producer of Bollywood movies and owner of a chain of fashion institutes across the country. Change of place had become mandatory to catalyse the process of forgiving and forgetting. She wanted a break; moreover she wanted time to think for herself and her life ahead.

Dr Verma was a man she always wished her father would emulate. He took care of Rihana but never asked her anything about Veer. Though in his mid-fifties, Dr Verma looked younger than his age. With a round face and a double-chin, he looked like a cuddly teddy bear. He was affectionate, generous, patient and sensitive to Rihana's predicament. Older people always carry a lot of experience behind them and that is reflected in their words and actions.

Dr Verma had once told Rihana, 'There is nothing more lucrative for a woman than a husband caught red-handed. You can rule Veer for the rest of your life.'

Rihana had then replied, 'Uncle, I never wanted to rule Veer. I wanted to spend a quality life with him. You know, one should be careful what one wishes for. Sooner or later, the wish comes true. I wanted to be out of a relationship with Veer. I wished it long back, and even in between, when I assumed things were improving, they were actually getting worse. My wish had been granted... I'm glad that I got a valid and legitimate reason to get out of this relationship.'

Dr Verma wanted to ensure what Rihana was thinking, more for her sake than his curiosity, 'But you could have got out of this relationship whenever you wanted. Why did you stay that long?'

'We are often caught in the webs woven by us and once entangled, we start extricating ourselves. This situation is uglier.'

'Does that mean that you have decided to leave Veer?'

'I'm aware that a divorce will be uglier, and so will also be my life ahead,' answered Rihana.

'Why do you say that, Rihana? It'll be ugly only if you want it to be. You are young and there is a whole lifetime ahead of you. But you must be sure as to why you want to divorce Veer,' asked Dr Verma.

'Uncle, his behaviour, habits, character, passions, and attitudes are a reflection of his instincts and instincts are deep rooted, like the roots of a tree. If you try to fiddle with the roots of the tree, it dies. You know what I mean?'

Dr Verma nodded and Rihana continued, 'And you know what uncle, my grandfather's last wish was that I don't end up wrongly paired. If I realise that the pain would be much more than the happiness, I should let it go. He had told me this while I was still too young to understand his words, while I did not have marriage on my mind...but now I think back and know what he had wanted me to do. He had wanted me to live...and happily so.'

Dr Verma looked at her affirmatively and said, 'Veer will not divorce you so easily. He would like to stabilize things and everybody will support him, because keeping relationships is a better option. Plus, he knows that if the marriage breaks now, the entire onus will be on him. He doesn't seem like the guy who could endure it on his ego.'

What he said made perfect sense, but she was confused about keeping relationships just for convenience. 'Do you also feel the same?' she asked.

Rihana knew that Dr Verma himself had a broken marriage. She had never seen him interact with his wife and the only reason they were not legally separated was because of their children and the institutes they owned. Children and money are the two most important reasons that keep a marriage going in the absence of love, and Rihana, fortunately or unfortunately, had neither at stake.

Rihana confided in Dr Verma, explaining to him her predicament. She made it clear that her parents were not overly enthusiastic about her returning home. And she also saw the value of a woman who was in trouble with her own husband. Practically pushed to a corner, Rihana told Dr Verma that she had made up her mind to leave Veer. But clearly, being the woman, her family's sensibilities would get hurt if she left.

'Blame it on society, Rihana. These self-imposed regulations stifle us and yet we follow them,' said Dr Verma, almost convinced that Rihana had seen a glimpse of the road ahead of her and needed some support to be able to make the right choice.

Dr Verma was not only modern in thoughts and lifestyle, but also progressive with respect to traditions and values.

Meanwhile, Veer on the other end, was trying everything possible to get Rihana back in his house. He had almost fallen at Rihana's mother's feet and pleaded for Rihana's comeback. But she wasn't able to analyze the reasons behind such a behaviour. Nevertheless, her experience told her a man had two extremes of a personality: if Veer could prostrate, he could also get extremely edgy and behave erratically. Although she knew Veer was capable of trouble, but in her confusion about Veer's behaviour and reasons behind it, Rihana's mother took pity on her son-in-law and gave him Rihana's address in Mumbai.

'I'm not meeting Veer, Mom. Why did you give him the address? Now he will come here and sit on my head! Didn't I tell you I needed some time with myself to decide what I want to do? Why are you behaving like an enemy to me?' Rihana voice was touching the roof while fighting with her mother over the phone.

Rihana's mother wished Veer and Rihana to be together. Her motive was the same when she stood guarantee for Veer's behaviour while asking Rihana to get married to him. But as the saying goes, 'The motive doesn't serve the purpose,' and now the old woman knew not what to do. She juggled between some very strong inherent forces: the will to see her daughter happy, Rihana's wish to move out of Veer's life and throw him out of hers, social pressure of having a divorced daughter, and Veer's histrionics which she was unable to gauge.

Veer came to Mumbai, so Rihana *had* to meet him. But she agreed to do so in the presence of her uncle; she wanted to ensure a witness for every meeting now as no one had believed her earlier. When Veer asked Rihana to come back to him, Dr Verma asked

Veer one question, 'Veer, a marriage is based on trust and you've always breached it. Why should Rihana live with you?'

Veer quipped, 'So that I can build it again.'

'Build it again and break it again,' whinged Rihana.

The meeting came to nothing, but Veer frequently visited Rihana to convince her. Rihana saw no difference in his behaviour, though. Even now he was asking her to be back, and not assuring her or soothing her insecurities. Rihana loved her family, and had gotten into this disaster of a marriage because of that love. But she had decided to take things into her hands now and had to be careful. She didn't want to hurt her family, but she could not tolerate living with Veer anymore.

Raj, in the meantime, discovered Rihana's separation from Veer and felt an opportunity knocking at his door. He found her contact details and got in touch with her again. Rihana didn't have any regrets regarding Raj; she just had her lessons learnt the hard way and didn't want a repetition of her mistakes.

In a world shrunken to a click, thanks to Google, finding someone was not a problem. Moreover, Raj had been in touch with all her friends, though she could never understand why. She had left him behind when he refused to stand by her. She did not blame him for her predicament, but did not want to make the same mistake again. She firmly believed in black or white, a yes or a no. The shades of grey were difficult to comprehend. He called her up and told her that he had come to Mumbai for work and figured she was around, and would like to catch up. Rihana agreed to meet Raj over a cup of coffee and a lot happened over that coffee.

She had loved Raj once, but she loved herself more to let go of her respect now. She wasn't willing to lose herself once again. With these thoughts set firmly in her mind, she went to meet Raj.

Raj saw Rihana walk into the coffee house and immediately stood up. He offered her a chair and she sat next to him, looking at him straight in the eyes to know what was going on in his mind.

Raj took Rihana's hand in his and spoke gently, 'I know you've gone through hell, Rihana, and I'm sorry that I left you then. I wasn't sure if I was ready to take on the responsibility of a committed relationship... If I knew Veer would behave like this, I would...'

'So, are you ready now?' Rihana asked him in a sarcastic tone.

'Yes, I am!' He replied with his head bowed down while he still held Rihana's hand. He lifted his face to see her response, but her expressions were as cold as the North Pole.

Rihana was now more careful, not to mention sceptical of men by default. She understood the proposal to be some kind of a trap for her. Suspicion had eaten away at her innocence and she didn't know if that was a curse or a boon.

She took her hand away from Raj's and said firmly, 'Sorry, my friend, it's too late now. I've moved on. You once advised me to form an opinion about Veer myself. I have used the same pearls of wisdom to form an opinion about you too.'

Raj looked taken aback; he hadn't seen this coming, 'And, may I ask what that opinion is?' asked Raj.

'Like my life, my opinions also belong to me. I refuse to share them with you. But I will say this for sure: your apology is not enough for the precious months of my life wasted in such torture. It is not enough, Raj. In a way, what you did was betrayal; what we had shared was special. At least to me. And yet, you cared more about what society thought and the possible repercussions to your life than commit to our relationship. It was devastating for me because I found you and lost you in a wink of time.'

'You are leaving Veer because he was with another woman. Why be so judgmental when you did the same with me.' Rihana looked up at him slowly as he mentioned this, and didn't stop just here, 'What if Veer comes to know of this?' He sounded desperate; to care Rihana or convince her into being with him.

'So that's the plan, han? I am so glad you said this, Raj. It's you who had once told me that everything in your life has a span and if you stretch it beyond that, it'll only give you pain. Our span is over. I can never be with you again,' replied Rihana and closed another chapter of her life. This closure was necessary for her. That day, as she moved out of the coffee shop, she took a firm step to move on too.

Rihana was in a state where she could have taken help, but not sympathies or guilt. Raj had decided to find her and confess all this not because of love, but guilt at having made her suffer his inaction. And on top of it was sympathy, and *that* she did not want. And she did not want Raj to look back later in life and feel like a hero who had rescued her and therefore done her this huge favour. He would then be dictating the shots in their marriage, not from a place of love but from a place of the knight in shining armour. She didn't want to be the fairy tale Rapunzel waiting for her prince charming to rescue her. She only wished if girls were not narrated stories of a prince rescuing the damsels in distress, they would not have waited for miracles to happen but instead been a little more realistic.

Rihana now welcomed a new life. She had no clue how to bring it about. But she knew that the first step was to acknowledge and open the doors of her heart to new possibilities.

Rihana was enjoying her new work in Mumbai; it was her passion for colours. Designing, cutting, stitching and giving form to raw cloth gave her a lot of happiness and came naturally to her. She took any work that came her way. While working, she was also trying to get better at designing by learning from senior designers who were employed by her uncle for some of the actresses. She was a creative person and the designs she prepared got picked up for a few Bollywood actresses. That was the tipping point in her career's launching stage. With her designs getting appreciated everywhere, her creativity blossomed under the shower of compliments. But then came the time for the businessman in her to act and do the right kind of marketing to create a brand image. The tangibles were created by her; she now had to work on the intangibles. In any field, from Physics to Management to Medicine to Psychology, 'It is always the unseen which is more consequential than the seen'.

Rihana's designs were really liked by one of the actresses in a movie produced by Dr Verma. Her name was Himangi and she would always come to her for party wears. That was the right time for Rihana to seek her uncle's help. She wanted to launch a brand of hers in the name of 'Rihana's' and there was nobody else who could have guided her better than Dr Verma. When Rihana went to her uncle seeking his assistance and advice, he patted her, 'It's a good decision, but why don't you take some professional qualification also. Till now, you are doing it without any training. I am aware you were teaching students some basics of design but knowing more about the technical aspects and fabrics will enable you to do a better job. Why don't you just hop into one of my institutes?' advised Dr Verma.

Dr Verma's fashion institute had branches all over India and was considered one of the best in India. Dr Verma knew well that she was a hardworking and talented girl. To grow in the same profession wasn't a choice but a mandate for her. Dr Verma on his part was doing indirect marketing for his institute by letting a rising star be a part of his institute. Rihana agreed to enrol in his college and in turn he promised to help her with her brand launch. For six months after that, Rihana attended college in the mornings and worked in the evenings to create designs for people. What she missed was a brand image. Fashion industry, like any other industry is dominated by the big fish. These big fish don't share their space; and if someone enters, it is eaten up by the big fish.

New entrants in the fields of fashion, politics and movies required a Godfather. A fashion institute owner and a producer of Bollywood movies was a perfect combo that Rihana had in hand. Rihana was a hardworking girl, and was at the right place, at the right time, in the right hands. That was all that mattered.

While Rihana was whole heartedly devoted to her passion, Veer kept trying to get her back by convincing her parents. He even sent her gifts and love notes to win over her. Veer's calls acted as a distraction for her, especially when she was trying to focus to build a new life for herself. He was like a force pulling her backwards. By now, Rihana had shifted into a rented house as she preferred staying alone. Though she was left alone, she was not at all lonely. She was in the process of discovering herself and it couldn't be done in the company of others.

One such day, when Rihana was resting after a long day, Vikram called her up. As his name flashed on her phone screen, she was taken back to the phone bills he had handed over to her in Delhi, the same bills that had made her wonder at Veer's loyalty the first time.

He sounded polite and calm, 'I was sad to hear about you and Veer. I hope you are doing fine.'

'I'm doing well Vikram. How are you and Renu doing? And was it a baby boy or girl?'

'It's a baby girl,' replied Vikram through a smile, 'I am surprised you remembered.'

'Congratulations for the little angel! So now you have to be a responsible father. You know Vikram, when one thinks of baby girls, one conjures up an image of satin ribbons and frilly frocks. One perceives softness, love and care. My mother would prevent me going out to play because of the fear that I would fall and get bruised. I'm sure you will protect your daughter and face all odds to give her happiness.'

In the past few months, Rihana had understood how daughters made men human. As fathers, they fought for their daughter's well being and protected her. But the day she got married, they cried. Not because she was getting married, but because they would no longer have any control over them. All their deeds or misdeeds with all the women in the world flash before their eyes and then they pray to God that whatever they did to any woman should not be repeated with their daughter. That is when they metamorphose into a human being. Daughters did that to men.

For quite some time, there was silence akin to a graveyard over the phone. And after a pause, Vikram said, 'Rihana, Veer is suffering. He misses you. I agree he made a mistake, but men do much worse. He is apologetic and wants you back. There is a difference between a man and a woman. A woman is an epitome of forgiveness and love. You have to look after Veer's self respect and in turn, yours. Please consider his apology.'

Rihana knew this would come sometime soon, and had been prepared for it all along. 'How do you know that he has not done much more, Vikram? I kept that much more under wraps.

I showed my love and forgiveness there. Men want to claim that they are men but forget that the need to be a human being first. I am sure you do know that human beings don't have gender discrimination.'

Vikram was about to say something, but Rihana cut him in between, 'Do you know he even accused me of having a fling with you?'

She let it sink in, but she knew she had hit the nail on the head. 'What wrong did I do with you, Vikram? Let's get real. You were more vulnerable than me when you came home that day, remember? If I wanted, you wouldn't have ever said no. But I controlled myself; not for myself, but for Veer. I was not protecting my self-respect, but Veer's. I defeated you to let Veer win. Just because I've caught him red handed, it is his ego that is making him come back to me. I have done everything to protect his ego.'

'I don't know what to say, Rihana,' Vikram sounded stumped.

'And then, tell me, from the entire bunch of his friends, why did he approach only you to convince me? Especially when he had once accused me of entertaining you the wrong way? Especially when he made sure to tell my family and his that I was salivating over other men... He knows that once I get convinced by you, he can accuse me again of having a relationship with you. I'm sorry, Vikram, but as of now...*I'm not convinced.*' Rihana made sure Vikram saw her reason and stayed out of it.

After listening to Rihana, Vikram couldn't justify Veer's case anymore and gave up.

Veer was behaving like a baby whose toy had been snatched, and he cribbed only to have that toy back.

Rihana's father stayed away from this matter but her mother still encouraged the relationship, dreading the impending divorce. 'If you ever get a divorce, I will die,' she often told her daughter.

Rihana had been blackmailed once and fell into the trap of marriage. But she also loved her mother like she loved none else. She knew her mother would not give up on it till she agreed. So, for her sake and with the determination to test the waters for everyone to see this time, she convinced herself to give Veer another chance. After all, everybody deserved a second chance.

Twisted Feelings

Rihana agreed to giving Veer another chance, but with a strict condition to herself to not be influenced by emotional blackmail, by anyone. Her term at the institute in Mumbai was ending, and she took a small break before plunging into her brand.

Coincidentally, one of Veer's friends in Jaipur was getting married, Rihana's mother had told her. She thought it would be a good time to go. She could observe Veer's behaviour in public and also his habit of drinking.

She took a flight to Jaipur and landed straight at her in-laws' house. It was despairing for her to see her father-in-law in a pathetic condition. He was in depression for no fault of his. She felt pity for him, but was helpless. She had told herself to not fall for emotions this time; so while she cared for him and spoke to him endearingly, she did not let that affect her view about Veer.

It was Ravi Poonia's wedding, the same guy who had been humiliated by Veer for hitting on Rihana. When she realised this, Rihana went up to the dais and shook hands with Ravi and his pretty partner. She looked at Veer from the corner of her eyes and saw his mouth break into an uneasy smile. He had been drinking, but in control. He had been talking to women, but with great effort to keep it in check.

After the wedding, Rihana spoke to Veer and asked him to be patient. She needed some breathing time to take the exams for the course she had just finished. She also shared with him her plans for her future. But Veer had a problem with it.

'Why do you want to be in Mumbai? You can be with me in Kolkata; the new office is all set. We can start a new life,' proposed Veer.

Rihana wanted to be financially independent by having something of her own. She didn't want her father's support, or her husband's if she intended to stay with him.

Veer wasn't sure about the "financially-independent-woman" image that Rihana was carrying; but she had never been so sure of anything more in her life.

Rihana's father-in-law was happy to see them together, and hoped for Rihana's wounds to heal. Rihana was happy because her father-in-law was happy. Rihana stayed with them for a few days and left for Mumbai thereafter, while Veer flew to Kolkata. She stopped to meet her parents only for a few hours, that too because she wanted to see her Dadi.

The old woman was ecstatic to see Rihana, fresh as a flower again. She told her a simple thing, 'Rihana, do what makes you happy. This life is so precious; I wouldn't want you to look back with any regrets. And about people who scare you about society and relationships, always remember that you come first, my dear. Everyone else will eventually come by.'

After Rihana left Jaipur, she jumped into her work with great gusto. Any business in the world required maintaining good relations and Rihana was adept at that. She had made many friends with whom she interacted and went out. Rihana had a larger social acceptability due to her attitude, good looks and confidence in herself. Her uncle appreciated her as she was always well and exclusively dressed.

Appreciating Rihana's dressing sense, her friend Avinash once told her, 'When the world looks at you dressed, they will surely know that you have a smart sense of clothing. I am sure you can create riches out of rags, Rihana. You know those designers who dress weirdly enough themselves and claim to be superb in the art of designing? I am sure people look through them. You... are something!'

Rihana was elated to hear this, that too coming from Avinash. He was an IPS officer, the Deputy Commissioner of Police to be more precise. At around thirty-three years old, they had met in one of the fashion shows that Rihana was showcasing her designs in and he was one of the chief guests. When conversing with him, Rihana was surprised to meet a cop who had such abundant knowledge about fashion and the fashion industry.

He asked Rihana, 'How do you design so well?'

To which Rihana promptly replied, 'I just add a little bit of passion to fashion.'

'I agree, passion takes you a long way and I'm sure that you'll go a long way. With passion you never cease to grow...but make sure that your reasons hold the reins,' Avinash went into a philosophical mode.

But Rihana enjoyed her conversations with him. She was charmed by this man in uniform. She had many friends, but she loved interacting with Avinash and that feeling was mutual, thanks to their thought frequency matching. They spoke about everything from high heels to high crimes in the city. Both of them were so comfortable with each other that Rihana once shared her lesbian fantasy with him. He was slightly taken aback and asked her if she had always felt like doing it. She had replied in the negative, saying the need for a partner and the disappointment with her man had jointly driven her to such a thought.

Avinash knew about Veer but never formed an opinion about anyone. He believed that whatever happens between a husband and a wife, only they know and that was no one else's business. Moreover, people joining the civil services have a greater degree of common sense and Avinash was no exception.

He further proved it by saying, 'You know, many women experience such tendencies because of nasty experiences with their men? They perceive women to be more understanding and soft. And let me tell you, a woman only knows a woman's body. Also, the next time you are living that fantasy in your head, please invite me.'

Rihana laughed out loud, to Avinash's utter amusement, because he never thought the petite Rihana was able to conjure such roaring laughter. That was the first time after her marriage that she was laughing so whole heartedly. And as usual, her laughter was contagious; Avinash laughed with her. She found that she understood Avinash very well and he also seemed to understand her well. She found that time passed very quickly in their togetherness. He gradually became her best friend.

Meanwhile, Veer and Rihana started attending social events for each other, but it was more of a social obligation. Veer then decided to take a month's leave and stay with Rihana. During his stay at Mumbai, Veer would snoop on Rihana's whereabouts from the cook, the security guard and even her maid. He was trying to gather information against her to get even, she knew. Rihana also knew pretty well that relationships were not about getting even, but to let the other partner win. When a relationship is weakened by breach of trust, it doesn't take time to break. Veer and Rihana were walking on a thin rope with no support. The foundation was shaken.

One day when Rihana returned from her work, her cook told her, 'Madam, sir was asking me questions about you. Who comes to the house and who is your best friend. Madam, I don't know anything so didn't tell him. But he wasn't ready to believe me and told me that I was lying. Madam I don't lie. If you're not happy with my work, I'll leave, but I don't lie.'

After listening to all that rubbish, Rihana got very upset and stormed into the room where Veer was watching TV.

'Veer, has the world run short of meaningful things to do, or are you just considering asking maids about your wife as your favourite time pass?' He continued staring at her blankly and she stormed, 'Why are you just looking for a reason to leave me? Are you really suspicious or just digging for an excuse to soothe your ego and guilt conscience? If you don't want to be with me, just ask for a divorce. I'm more than willing for that, and you know it pretty well. I thought you were changing, isn't that what you told me? But I see you back to square one.... Oh no! Lower than that.'

'What are you talking about Rihana?' He said perfectly calmly, 'Your cook must be cooking up stories along with food. I didn't say anything. I love you and want you back in my life. I made a mistake, but can't be punished for it forever, now that I am totally dedicated to you. I can't afford to lose you. Please forgive me,' pleaded Veer.

Rihana was perplexed. She knew the cook won't tell lies for such a thing; what would she gain out of it! For all she knew, Veer could have proceeded with the divorce and started over with a brand new life. Rihana never wanted to be with him and now she had valid reason to do so. She sat down to isolate the reasons. She knew that he didn't love her and he didn't want sex from her either. Then why was he sticking around? Probably, Veer could not take rejection. Rejection in many ways is louder than acceptance, especially to the person who is rejected. His social insecurities, with a pinch of ego, were making him cajole her back into the dead relationship. Rihana wanted to get rid of him, but then thought of her mother's anguish who didn't want the relationship between Veer and Rihana to end. Veer's family was also going through the same predicament. They kept themselves from speaking to Rihana because they understood her misery. And giving her time was the only option they had. Moreover, it was politically correct as their son had faltered by having an extra-marital affair; but for Rihana, he had faltered much more than that.

Rihana hadn't witnessed any change in Veer's behaviour in all this time and it wasn't even expected. She was looking for something new on which she could base her relationship, if getting out wasn't the option.

Where Rihana could not figure out Veer's motives to have her back in his life, there he had his priorities fixed. Veer could not think beyond the idea of the husband owning the wife, like a landowner owns the land. He was impatient to harvest Rihana for a good crop. Without Rihana, he would be left socially insecure, denied the right to beget progeny, would fail at keeping his hereditary line going and would miss a collaborating partner who could uplift his career. Now, his only aim was to have a child with Rihana so that it could keep her bound to him and he could keep the settling of scores with her for later.

A man rejected for his sexual incompetence by a woman is like a wounded snake waiting in the wings to strike its exterminator.

Veer was undoubtedly potent; Rihana was unhappy with him because he never understood her needs. She wouldn't care so much if it was only about her physical needs. All she needed was a little time and a little love. She wanted a little pampering with a little acknowledgement. She wanted a little chat with a little bit of listening. All these 'little' things were not too big a deal; but maybe Veer didn't think so.

Now, while Rihana was out in the day, Veer would while away his time at home watching TV, sending her messages and looking around the house. In one such expedition around the house, he found the bunch of spare keys for all the doors inside the house.

Veer and Rihana stayed in different rooms but Veer behaved like the desperate alien who wanted to copulate in order to have progeny of her own alien species. Veer was carrying the same desperation and would have killed for it.

After retiring for the night, and before going to sleep, Rihana would carefully lock her door from inside. On one such night, Veer used the keys of her bedroom door he had found to sneak into her bed. He nestled against Rihana and whispered in a soft tone, 'Love, I miss you a lot. Give me another chance.' Saying this, he kissed her on her lips.

Rihana was bewildered. Veer was warm and gentle when he started kissing her, but it soon changed to biting, and later into monstrous force which made Rihana's lips bleed. Rihana screamed in pain but Veer didn't stop. He removed only her underpants forcefully and hurriedly took off his boxers. Rihana tried to push him off her, but wasn't strong enough to do so. He clutched both her hands with his strong hold and got on top of her. Rihana could not breathe due to his heavy weight on her. She wriggled, twisted and turned her body in pain, but Veer didn't stop till he filled her with his semen. Her brain told her what Veer wanted to do, and she made a mental note of taking an emergency contraceptive pill soon after. Though she could take care of that, she was severely damaged physically and mentally. She just sat and wept, while Veer didn't seem to have realized his mistake also.

'Why are you crying? You always wanted sex and I'm giving it to you,' Veer justified his actions.

'Do you want an orgasm? I can give you one...' asked Veer.

Rihana was disturbed and didn't say anything. She was tender like a flower, and Veer had strewn her petals.

Rihana spoke to her mother about the incident the very next day and her agony of being in that relationship with Veer. Her mother promptly chided Veer and instructed him to take control of things more maturely. She also asked him to go back to his own house and let Rihana be. She was angry that Veer had let her down, yet again.

Veer called up Rihana's mother and apologized for his actions. He wriggled and pleaded to allow him to be with Rihana. And she being the socialite mother, once again took pity on him. After all, Rihana was his wife and Veer had a right to do what he did. No doubt, he needed Rihana's consent for exercising that right, but she was sure her could work on that.

Rihana was doubly sure now that she could not give any more chances to Veer to make things up to her. That was not happening! But she needed some support to wriggle free of his clutches... some support the power of which Veer could not challenge. And in Avinash she had found a friend for life.

She knew that Avinash was too much of a gentleman to ask any questions about her marital life but she also knew that he was caring enough to be curious. And the rumour mills must have been working overtime on Veer and Rihana for Avinash to be totally clueless.

On one of their many chats, Rihana decided to clear the air. She wanted Avinash to know everything about her. In four straight hours, she ran Avinash through the marathon of her tumultuous marriage. He only listened sagely and didn't speak a word until she had finished. When she had poured her heart out, he had only one thing to say to her, 'Rihana, you are too special to deserve such shoddy treatment. It's plain and simple. Get out and get out now, before you lose your battle and strength.'

By now Rihana had concluded that her parents, in-laws and the society would not let her come out of this relationship, no matter how many times she clicked pictures of her bruised self and showed it to others. She could never speak about her sexual frustrations lest she be tagged as a whore. If she didn't act, and act appropriately, she would have to deal with Veer's nonsense for the rest of her life. She had to think of something that got her out of this relationship quickly and forever.

♀

Veer joined Rihana for a trip planned by Rihana's friend Shipra. She, in turn, ensured that Avinash was also invited. They had conversations running over WhatsApp. They intended to holiday in Coorg, a hill station in Karnataka. Rihana wasn't very keen to begin with, but then she thought it would be a good retreat. Plus, Avinash had agreed to come along; that would ensure her safety. This was just as she had wanted. Veer had no objections and was more than willing.

Coincidentally, Ravi Poonia and his wife were returning from their long honeymoon in Maldives and told Veer that they'd be in Mumbai. Veer told them of his trip and asked them also to join. Avinash's aunt owned a farmhouse in Coorg, so the stay wasn't a problem. Avinash, on his part, made all arrangements, but backed out at the last moment on account of an important case needing him in town. Veer insisted that he came, as it made no sense for them to go to someone's house without the host. After a lot of persuasion from Veer, Avinash finally agreed. Rihana wanted this to happen. When things have to happen, everything falls in place.

The next morning, they met at the Mumbai airport – Avinash, Rihana, Veer, Ravi and his wife Noor – and took a flight to Bangalore. Shipra and her husband Nikhil met them at the Bangalore airport directly, from where they hired a cab for Coorg. It was a five hour journey and the newlyweds were happily enjoying the drive. Veer sat in front and kept the driver awake; the other six on the back seats chatted away. Rihana had a tough time because of motion sickness, but Avinash kept her occupied with his interesting conversations about dresses and designs. Veer was concentrating on the road ahead and wasn't really paying any attention to others, except Rihana. She was suspicious of that gesture too; she knew Veer too well to take him on face value.

After a quick stretching out break, Veer took his seat in front and Avinash went to the back seat with Shipra and Nikhil. Rihana was left nestled in the middle with Ravi and Noor. She saw them cuddle in the seat. They were in the exploration stage of their relationship. Rihana felt oversexed looking at Ravi and Noor caressing each other. To divert her feelings, she took out her frustrations by drinking wine. By the time they all reached Coorg, she was drunk and out. Veer gave her support and put her to sleep in one of the rooms in the farmhouse.

Since everyone was tired of the journey, they all spent the night in their rooms, keeping adventure for the days to come. Avinash, by habit of his profession, was the first one to be up in the morning. Since Rihana had slept long, she was also up early. She was sitting out on a chair in the garden when she saw Avinash come to the water tap in the garden to wash his slippers. He looked at Rihana and said, 'Good morning beautiful! There is nothing like pooping in the open.'

'You went out in the open to poop? There are bathrooms in the house,' said Rihana astonished as if she had witnessed a UFO in the woods.

Avinash replied with a smile, 'Yes, there are three bathrooms in the house, but all of them are attached to the rooms *couples* are occupying. This is the only time I have felt bad about being single. And I didn't want to disturb any of you.'

While Rihana and Avinash were having that conversation, Veer came out and joined them. 'Hangover?' he asked Rihana; she nodded.

'The best way to get over a hangover is to start drinking again. Should I get some wine? We have some home-made wines in the farm,' asked Avinash.

Veer chuckled and Rihana hit Avinash playfully on his arm. In the meantime, everyone got up and the servants laid out a brunch comprising exotic dishes. Everybody on the table enjoyed a sumptuous meal and then headed for a city tour. This time, Ravi drove and Noor helped navigation through her Google maps app. While Shipra and Nikhil occupied their favourite seats at the back, Rihana was nestled between Veer and Avinash in the middle seat.

Coorg holidays are usually a good dose of relaxed drives through lush greenery and fresh air with plenty of coffee and spice plantations along the way. So the gang resorted to drinking again. Avinash bought a ginger wine for Rihana, while everybody else preferred beer. Rihana only had a taste for wine and believed in Martin Luther's quote, 'Beer is made by men, wine by God.' She was almost a bottle down and felt tipsy, but so did everyone else. Veer was compensating for the previous day and got drunk. Driving under these circumstances was a little dangerous, so they all parked the car and sat in a small tea shack.

Veer was talking to the *chai wala* to know more about the history and geography of the place, leaving his drunken wife with a drunken man. The ugliest and the most beautiful mistakes happen in a drunken state. Rihana, on her part, knew that she wasn't making any mistakes. She gathered all her courage and held Avinash's hand. Avinash looked into her face with complete understanding. She had never felt so complete in her life. Or maybe it was the wine. Rihana tickled his hand, circling the palm with her finger nail. That intimacy between them had grown out of understanding and she knew exactly what she was doing. Veer sensed that there was a hunter around, but failed to know who it was – Avinash or Rihana? He waited like a cameraman with a sixth sense for action to happen so that he could capture it.

Ravi suggested going back to the farmhouse, now that the tea had brought him back to his senses, good enough to drive. A bonfire seemed like a good idea.

Everybody got in the car and Avinash made his first attempt to touch Rihana. It was a rush of energy that flowed from Avinash's hand to Rihana's body. It was filled with excitement, fear and wine that made the ambience even more interesting. Avinash had ignited the fire, but she was literally playing with it in Veer's presence. Rihana was burning with desire, the desire that was only known to Avinash and Rihana. As soon as they reached the farmhouse, Noor went inside to take a shower while Rihana, Avinash and Ravi made arrangements for the bonfire. Veer was nursing a headache so he went back to the room to catch some sleep. Shipra and Nikhil went around the farmhouse to explore the surroundings. Rihana and Avinash waited for Noor to come out and after the newly-weds were engrossed with each other, they sneaked out into the outhouse under the pretext of collecting wood for the bonfire. No one saw them for a while.

As soon as they were inside the outhouse, Avinash held Rihana close and kissed her on the lips. Rihana responded with equal passion. Avinash took Rihana's sweater off and unfastened her bra. Her shimmering ivory breasts popped and the fleshly monsters quivered with thirst. Looking at them, even God would have turned into a devil. Avinash was so mesmerised, he didn't know what to do with them. On Rihana's instructions, he took off his shirt and brought her close once again to kiss her. He began exploring her exquisite beauty, little by little. As his hands roved freely on her back, her nails dug into his, inching him closer to her. Rihana moaned with pleasure; her moans turned to exquisite cries and the cries turned to disaster. Veer entered the outhouse only to discover his topless wife in the hands of another man. He was storming with rage. He shouted and screamed like a baby whose toy had been broken into pieces. It was worse than death for him. There was betrayal, because there was trust first. Rihana had shattered that trust. Veer sat down on the floor and wept while Rihana put her clothes back. Avinash went out to light a cigarette, leaving Rihana and Veer alone. She came close to Veer and tried to make him stand up. He got up and slapped Rihana hard. Avinash rushed in and held Veer's hand obstructing the second slap.

'Let's behave like mature individuals. No violence,' Avinash meant business.

Veer couldn't have messed around with a cop and Avinash was aware of that fact. He could have buried Veer in the farmhouse alive and no one would ever know.

Veer dashed out of the outhouse and went straight to his room. Ravi and Noor followed him to know what had really happened. Shipra had heard a bit of the commotion and now stood facing Rihana, not saying a word. She just came up to Rihana and held her in an embrace. 'Rihana, whatever happens is for the best.' Avinash lit another cigarette and went back to his room. On Shipra's request, Nikhil shared the room with Veer and Rihana spent a restful night in Shipra's room.

The next day, Veer flew to Jaipur to place the matter before his family. He took Ravi and Noor with him, perhaps as witnesses.

Avinash drove Rihana and the others to the airport and took a flight back to Mumbai.

Shipra knew Rihana enough to not judge her; she wished her luck and left with Nikhil. Once they were left to themselves, he broke that silence and asked her,

'Why did you ask me to do this, Rihana? You're in a mess.'

'No, Avinash. I'm, in fact, *out* of the mess now. All thanks to you!'

'I know this went as per plan for you, but what will you get out of this?' enquired Avinash.

'You'll know soon enough. Let's say I am also waiting to see what all it gets me.'

Almost a Free Bird

Rihana's father called her up this time, asking for an explanation. She was glad that her father had finally decided to intervene. She confessed her crime, but the fact that it was planned was to be between her and Avinash alone.

There were no calls from Veer. When Rihana was *ordered* to fly to Jaipur, she told her mother matter of factly, 'Mom, I made a mistake, I'm sorry. I just got carried away.'

She was blunt and emotionless.

'You've put us to shame. How could you do such a thing? You've demeaned our name. What will we tell Veer's parents? This is just atrocious...' Rihana's mother went on and on and on.

Rihana's mother asked her to apologise to Veer also. So the same day, Rihana went to Veer's house with her parents and offered her apology. Veer, as she had expected, wanted to be loud and bring out his anger.

'Do you want to get married to Avinash?' he asked her.

'No, Veer! You are my husband and I can't think of it. Please let's forget all this and start a new life. I'm sure we can put this behind us,' Rihana feigned.

Veer knew that Rihana was called to Jaipur by her mother, so that's whom he addressed.

'See what your daughter has done. She has been sleeping around like a whore and tarnishing the family's name,' shouted Veer at Rihana's mother.

Rihana just stood there with an apologetic look and saw history repeat itself.

'I had asked you to get your daughter back. Why did she have to go to another man? Wasn't I enough for her?' He turned to Rihana almost venomously, 'You fallen woman, go and ask that girl Ishika. She called me a tiger in bed. I screwed her eleven times and you always doubted my sexual competence.'

'Veer, I'm ready to leave everything and come to live with you. We can start a new life. I'm sure you can forgive me,' Rihana pretended to plead, yet again, knowing full well the waters were about to overflow soon.

Rihana's family joined her, but their pleas were genuine. Her mother had been pleading for quite some time now - first in front of her own daughter and now Veer.

Her mother was still hopeful of the relationship between Veer and Rihana. But she may as well have been hoping for a pig to fly and for hell to be a cool place. There were no conclusions to that meeting; it just ended with Veer's abuses. Rihana had a voice in her mind answer all his allegations with just as much venom, but kept her calm. She had to set herself free. Veer walked out of the house without giving any sermons.

Veer stopped talking to Rihana and set up his office in Kolkata. Rihana went back to Mumbai and started her usual work and continued to build her brand. Both the families kept quiet about the issue as they had nothing more to say. After a couple of months, Rihana received a divorce notice from Veer where he had accused Rihana of infidelity.

The envelope heralded her freedom; she didn't care what was written inside.

Rihana had finally earned it and she was now sure what Veer was made up of.

Rihana called up her mother and informed her about the divorce notice. Rihana's mother was shattered, and told her daughter in a broken voice, 'I see what you have done Rihana, and I see why.'

Rihana knew her mother had seen the world around her, but had never imagined she'd be able to look through her stunt. She told her mother she didn't want to fight the divorce, so she wanted to get in touch with Veer to consider a no-contest divorce by mutual consent.

Rihana's mother informed Veer about this and he called up Rihana, 'I cannot live with you anymore, Rihana. I need a divorce and I'd like to have it quick,' he said.

'Thank you, Veer. You've set me free.' She hung up after this.

Epilogue

R ihana dashed to her car and drove like a free bird out in the open sky. She ran up the few stairs in a rush and ended up ringing the doorbell, breathless. Avinash was quick to open the door. When he saw her, he hugged her like there was no tomorrow. Finally letting go of Rihana, Avinash looked into her face enquiringly. Rihana's voice was quivering with emotions when she said, 'Avinash, my divorce petition is through!'

Avinash was solemn for a minute and then asked her with much concern, 'What if Veer had really forgiven you?'

She replied with a smile, 'Where do you find such men who give equal status to women? And even if he had forgiven me, what do you think I should have done - continued a life of brutality, hate, lies and deceit only for a society that doesn't care a damn? Bear his children only to get further rooted into a world of unhappiness after finding more of his extra-marital affairs? Give justifications to the world that my children are the reason for my living with my husband where the truth would always be denied? This freedom has come to me at a cost, Avinash. I'll not waste it.'

Rihana and Avinash ordered their favourite food home and enjoyed her newfound road to freedom.

The divorce petition was filed by Rihana and Veer for a divorce through mutual consent. Rihana had fought enough and now wasn't prepared for a fight. She had won her battles already and let Veer get away without claiming any alimony.

Six months later, they met again for the final signature on the dotted line. Veer walked up to her after the procedure was over and said, 'Thank you for not making it messy, Rihana.'

She looked at Veer with a smile. In a contained and a soft tone she said, 'Thank *you*, Veer for giving me this freedom. You and I committed the same mistake and yet, you and the society expected me to forgive you without imbibing that virtue of forgiveness in yourself. You expected me to do something that you were never prepared to do yourself.'

He looked flushed, perhaps realising the depth of what she had just said. That's when she delivered the final blow: 'That girl called you a tiger in bed isn't it, Veer? Do you know a tiger lasts but a few seconds in a tigress? I only wish you lasted even that long. But honestly, that wasn't my problem. My problem was that you never bothered about things that bothered me. You proved your capacity to that girl eleven times, right?' His gaze was buried in his feet. 'I wish you had given me but eleven minutes of your day; eleven minutes of love, care, and togetherness. Only if you lived those eleven minutes with me, our relationship would have lasted a lifetime. Just those eleven minutes would have saved me from playing this whole act out; saved me from being the deliberate sinner.'